Stranger in a Small Town

Mike Murtha

LEGAL INFORMATION

ISBN: 1937391140
ISBN-13: 978-1-937391-14-0
eISBN: 978-1-937391-15-7

Designed, printed and distributed by Romeii, LLC.
Edited by Melissa Gilman
eBook conversion and distribution by Romeii, LLC.
Visit our website at ebooks.romeii.com

Table of Contents

INTRODUCTION

Imagine if you lived in a big city and you embraced all of its fine arts and culture. Now you and your family are forced to move to a small town in Iowa because of a job transfer. This is what happens to the Williams family from New York City. The statue of Liberty in the New York Harbor always seems to promise a better life for all who would be a part of this life style. The only thing that resembles a towering statue in Burton, Iowa is their water tower.

The story revolves around a slightly shy, fifteen year old boy who has to adapt to small town America after his family moves to the Midwest. The town puts more pride in their high school football team than they do in any kind of fine arts. With the adjustments of a new school, trying to meet new friends while fighting off a bully, Chris Williams discovers some talents he never knew he had. This discovery comes after stepping out of his comfort zone. After accepting changes, Chris finds this small town and his life very exciting in a completely different way than he would have ever imagined. Enjoy a story that captures the innocence of a young man and new discoveries of himself and a charming small town.

FORWARD

Writing a novel is something brand new to me, however this story has been in my head for over twenty years. After being encouraged by a close friend, my wife and a few others, I decided to try to put the story into print. My creative background is in performing music as well as writing songs. I am also a sign painter. I did find a few similarities in writing a novel and writing songs. The challenge of keeping your audience interested and engaged is one of those similarities. This resembles the feeling of performing music to a live audience. I've been a semi professional musician for nearly forty years. Thank God I never quit my day job! I have been fortunate in my musical career to have played with some real professionals. I hope you enjoy my first attempt at being a novel writer.

I would like to thank some people who helped me complete this long process of writing my first novel. The first person I would like to thank is my wife Debbie. This would not have happened without her. She helped me in so many ways from listening to my ideas to helping me write things properly. Thank you to my good friend Dan Woll who helped to keep me on task and also read the story with some constructive help. Thank you to Audrey Brown and Edna Knutson Bjorkman. Both of you had such good suggestions. Thank you to Ryan and Dan Murtha who took the time to read some of my early rough drafts. Thank you to my mother Arlys who also read the story in the early part of my process and encouraged me to keep going.

DEDICATION

I would like to dedicate this book to my mother Arlys. She has always encouraged me in everything I've ever tried to do. She has always been there through all my dreams and crazy ideas. She would listen to my thoughts and often times gave me the courage to try something different. She is everything a Mom should be but above that she is my close friend. Thank you, Mom. I love you!

Chapter One

Today Chris Williams' daily routine of school and life in New York took on a whole different meaning. He felt betrayed, lonely and fearful of the unknown. As he arrived for his freshman classes at Lincoln High, Chris was unable to hide his emotions.

His best friend, Joe said, "Chris, what's wrong? You look like something is really bugging you."

Chris replied, "I'm really bummed out. You are not going to believe this." Suddenly the bell rang for classes to begin.

As the two of them hurried to their room, Joe tugged on Chris's shirt sleeve and said, "Tell me what's going on?"

Chris blurted out, "We're moving!" Still hurrying to class, with Joe running behind, they arrived just in time.

Joe whispered across to Chris, "You're moving? Where?"

Chris replied bitterly, "The North Pole." Joe was totally confused and just shook his head. The two friends got very little out of their literature class that day.

Later, Chris stopped and said, "Joe, I'm sorry, I'm not being very nice here, so here's what's going on."

Then he told his best friend the whole story, that they were moving to Iowa. For the rest of the day they both were very quiet. As word got out to all of Chris's friends, it became a main topic of conversation the remaining days of school.

It all started the day before. Chris was watching his favorite TV after-school shows drinking a can of cola and munching on some chips, totally tuning out his ninth grade responsibilities. New York Lincoln High School and all its pressures were behind him for another day. He was counting the days when school would be over and summer vacation begins. It was May 28th. Only six more days and school would be out for the summer. Normally this time of day Chris paid little attention to his parents' conversation, but today was different. He couldn't believe what he was hearing.

He walked into the living room where his mom and dad were standing, facing each other with bewildered and concerned looks on their faces.

Chris said, "Dad, please tell me what I heard is a joke. You're kidding, right Dad?"

The confused look on his dad's face was still there, while Chris wore a worried smile. "No Son, I was going to tell you at supper tonight," replied his dad. "I'm stunned myself and so is your mother. Yes, I'm getting transferred. The company needs a plant manager in Burton, Iowa to take over operations."

Chris interrupted and said, "Operations of what, corn fields or pig farming? That's all there is in Iowa as far as I know. And just where is Burton, Iowa anyhow? And do we have to go with you?"

"Of course you do. This is a permanent transfer, and I'm not so sure how I feel about it either," replied his dad. "I do know this much, I need this job."

Chris asked, "How about my friends and school and my drama and theater, and my guitar? What about literature and all that stuff!"

His Dad said, "I thought you hated all those extra classes."

Chris replied, "I know but, but, they sure won't have classes like that in Iowa, will they?"

"Chris, don't forget your mother and I also grew up in New York. This will not be easy for any of us."

"What about my sister?" he asked. "Do they have any decent colleges in Iowa?"

"Chris, I don't think Vickie will have to leave Princeton University just because we are leaving New York," his Dad explained.

Chris was thinking to himself about the times his mom and dad would take him and his sister to some of the live theater shows downtown New York. Also the great restaurants they would frequent on some Friday nights, and the time they all saw a Broadway show to celebrate mom's birthday. Those things won't be in Iowa.

Cindy, Chris's mom, finally said, "Can I say something? What about me, Ben? My social club meetings, bridge parties, my book club and my tennis club, and all my friends, not to mention my love for the theater." As tears appeared on her face she turned and quickly said, "I need to make supper."

Cindy was a very pretty lady with slightly darker blond hair. She had somehow kept her slender figure after having two children and more than twenty plus years of marriage. Chris's sandy colored blondish hair came from his mother's side.

As they were eating supper, hardly a word was said until Chris asked, "I could stay here with my friend Joe and his parents, right?"

As Ben looked over the top of his glasses staring at his son, Cindy said, "We all have to talk this over and accept what's going on here. Your dad needs this job and we don't have a lot of choices."

Finally after a long silence, Chris asked "When do we have to be there, Dad?"

Ben replied, "We have to be there before August 10th. That will give you time to say good-bye here and get registered for school in Burton, Iowa."

Chris slid back in his chair and said, "I'm not hungry anymore. Can I be excused?"

As Cindy glanced over at Ben, her tears reappeared. Ben did not react because he was not an overly emotional person. Ben was a dark-haired slightly overweight man with glasses. It showed that he has been behind a desk for several years. He was still a handsome man but some grey hairs and a few extra pounds had appeared the last couple of years.

Chris usually felt carefree and exuberant on the last day of school, like he was free. But today it was different. It meant saying good-bye to some good friends and some teachers for perhaps the last time. At the end of the day, Chris took a final long look at the inside of his school and he felt very strange and sad. It was almost a feeling of rejection and of no longer being a part of all of this. Going to school had become so routine and that he took it for granted that he would always be there.

As tears clouded his eyes, Chris tried to hide it from those around him, but he couldn't hide it very well. Joe and Chris walked out of the school together. For years they always raced for about a block or so to see who was the fastest runner and Chris always won. It seemed odd that Joe always suggested they race but he never once won.

Perhaps it was a way for Joe to see if he was measuring up to Chris, but Chris never took it too seriously.

When Joe suggested they race again tonight, Chris just said he was not in the mood. The big lump in Chris's throat kept him from saying much of anything. When they got to Chris's house they went inside for a can of soda. "Chris," Joe said, "lighten up man, we got all summer to have fun."

"I know, but I've just got…. I don't know what you call it, but I guess it's pride," said Chris. "I'm proud to be from New York and all it represents. Its culture, history and all the cool things that are right here, like the time our school took the trip to see the Statue of Liberty. Or the time your parents took us to see the Empire State building. What I'm trying to say is it's cool to be from New York City. It's not cool to be from Iowa."

"How do you know that?" said Joe.

Chris just hung his head, shrugged his shoulders and said nothing.

Chapter Two

That summer was different. It was consumed with packing their things in boxes, cleaning the house and the storage area and watching the Realtors show their house to everybody who requested a tour. On July twenty-third the house was officially sold. The SOLD sign out front seemed to seal their fate and confirm the whole ugly reality for him. It also was the first time Chris actually got a little excited about moving. He was nervous about making new friends. He also was afraid he wouldn't like his new school. They probably didn't offer the classes that Chris liked—drama, theater, and classical guitar. Even though he often complained about those classes, he was actually an artsy person. He worried that they might not be offered in a small school, and that he would miss them. Even the class play he was in each year was a lot of fun. At one time he had hopes of being an actor or a director after college.

"Are some of these dreams a little too out of reach now?" he wondered . In spite of all those fears, there was still a certain amount of excitement with the big move.

As the moving vans drove off with all their belongings Chris looked at his watch, 10:15 August 1. He had two hours to say a final good-bye to his friends and the big city life. It was hard to do, but he promised he would be back sometime to see them. He sat quietly in the back seat as they drove off in the family Buick. The trip to Burton, Iowa was finally happening. His mom and dad had already made two brief trips to Burton but this was his first. In the previous visits they found and rented a house, and their furniture was supposed to arrive soon. Ben also got set up at his work. His job was challenging and interesting because he was in charge of a government plant that tested new energy sources, like ethanol, alcohol powered generators and wind powered generators.

After two full days of traveling it was finally in front of them—a sign that said "Welcome to Burton, Iowa. Population 2,061. Home of the Fighting Bulldogs".

"Dad," Chris asked, "What's that big tower for? The one that says 'Burton, Iowa' on it."

His dad said, "That's a water tower, and our house is just a little past the tower."

While driving up Main Street they passed by some old brick buildings, two taverns, and an aging grocery store. Across one street there was a large wooden town hall with peeling white paint and a faded wooden sign hanging out front. The town also had a post office, bank and hardware store. There was a large feed mill and farm service store on the edge of town. The streets were lined with large oak and maple trees, and there were flower boxes on the corners. People were walking on the sidewalks, giving a quick wave to anyone going by, and there were cars and trucks slowly driving down the streets. There was one stoplight in the middle of the town where two main highways intersected. They turned left to where their new home was located. As Chris got his first look at their new house, his first impression was a good one. It was a large white house with a big yard. In the driveway there was a basketball hoop above the garage door. It had a homey look. In the part of New York where they lived there wasn't room for a basketball hoop in the driveway, and a big yard was unheard of.

As they got out of the Buick his dad commented that the town felt like going back in time a few years when life was a little simpler and a little slower pace. He commented that this town has a peaceful charm to it.

His mom said, "Chris, come and see your new room."

"Hey Mom," said Chris," just slow down a little, I'm not a three year old! Give me a chance to look around."

The front of the house had a big white wrap-around porch. By the street there was a slightly cracked concrete sidewalk and a small grassy boulevard. Tall maple trees towered and covered part of the street with a shaded tunnel effect.

"I have to admit it seems peaceful," thought Chris. The whole area was so different than anything he was used to in New York City. He could actually hear birds singing. As Chris looked around a little more, he strolled into the house. The house had a simple charm to it. It had an open stairway and maple hardwood floors. Chris thought once again, "This looks better than I expected. It is kind of like what you would see in a movie." He was trying not to get his hopes up too high. From the looks of the main street, there was not a whole lot of anything special going on in this little one-horse town.

As Chris finished supper in their new home, his mom and dad noticed the emptiness in his face. The fear of starting over in a new neighborhood, and in a new school was hard to hide at this point.

Cindy said, "Chris, why don't you take a walk downtown, and take a look around. I think there might be a baseball game going on down at the end of Main Street."

"Mom, where would I go by myself?" said Chris. "I don't know anybody. I don't think I even want to get to know anybody just yet."

"Just try to work with us a little bit. This is no easier for us than it is for you. Just go and do something," she said.

So he wandered out the front door and found his way down the main street. One of the first things he noticed were the cars and pickup trucks just cruising up and down the streets. In New York, having your own car was nearly impossible, at least where he lived, most people rode the bus or the subway. If a person under twenty years old was driving a car it made people wonder if it was stolen. If a younger driver was seen, the stereo was always louder than the engine. Here the engines sounded great, like a hot rod you'd see in some old movie. Some of the people who were cruising up and down the streets were sure looking at him. Being a little self-conscious, Chris turned away. In doing so he felt uneasy, and really out of place.

As he kept walking down the street he found himself looking in the windows of the stores. All were closed now except the taverns. He found it interesting that a building that must have been a clothing store at one time was now a recycling center. Another building that must have been a market of some kind was now an apartment building. You could still see the faded lettering on the store fronts. Chris was trying to piece together his impressions of his new hometown, but found it hard to become comfortable yet with his new surroundings. It looked like a town that had struggled with changing times, but still retained its feel of the small town atmosphere.

Chris found his way to the end of Main Street. He quickly noticed the sounds of a sporting event. It was summer baseball. Apparently the local high school team was playing some other high school. As he walked through the parking lot, the sight of an older four-wheel-drive pickup caught his attention. When Chris looked at the cab he couldn't help but admire the old Ford truck hoisted high in the air. It had big over-sized tires on fancy wheels, and a shorter box. He was more interested in the old truck than the baseball game. Soon he found himself stepping up on the running board to get a good look at the inside of this modified hot rod truck. As he looked inside he noticed that it had an expensive stereo, a cool shifter, a gun rack and a can of chewing tobacco kind of hidden under a baseball cap. Chris got caught up in the moment and forgot he was a stranger in a small town on this hot summer evening. Quickly he was brought back to reality when he heard a loud voice from the baseball field. That voice was from a kid named Billy Snow.

He shouted out, "Hey you, you jerk! Get away from my truck unless you want me to kick your tail, ya nosey little twerp."

Laughter came from the crowd of people as they turned to see Chris trying to back away from the Ford truck.

The voice of Billy Snow once again shouted out, "Go on, get outta here before I chase you down like a dog!" Chris turned and ran a few steps.

Billy Snow was the first baseman on the team. He also played football and to some of the local people was singled out as special in this small town because of his athletic abilities. Billy was a stocky built, dark- haired kid with a little bit of a scruffy beard. He also had a bad complexion, round face and thick eyebrows. The high school football team was counting on Billy to help secure a championship this season. The team had been in a slump for a few years and some thought Billy was the future of their team for the upcoming year. Billy would be a senior, and was primed for the task.

Chris soon stopped running and walked slowly to the end of the parking lot. He felt embarrassed and rejected. As he walked toward the gate, again he heard Billy's gruff voice saying something to him, but this time he was close behind him. Chris wanted to say something back but just dropped his head and quickly ran away.

Chapter Three

It was nearly the end of August and Chris had not found any friends yet. His days were spent playing guitar by himself and reading. He had been active playing classical guitar and jazz in New York, but he felt like that belonged in New York. Burton, Iowa seemed too far removed from that level of music and for him to try to connect with any musician friends.

On the walls of Chris's bedroom he had posters of some of his favorite memories of New York. He had a picture of Yankee Stadium, some posters of Fender guitars, and one of Broadway. All of this seemed too distant from Iowa.

One day while playing guitar in the front room, Chris heard a voice outside the window. It was a pretty voice of a young girl singing along with the melody he was playing.

As he stopped playing to take a look he discovered a long-haired, teenage girl outside the window.

Chris stared in surprise, and she quickly said, "Don't stop playing now, you're just getting warmed up."

"How long have you been out there?" he asked.

The young girl answered, "Ah, well several days I guess."

Chris replied, "You don't mean you've been out there listening to me or spying on me for several days?"

She quickly said, in a humble voice, "I couldn't help but notice you are new in town and I thought I'd walk over this way because you hardly ever come out of your house. I walked by here a couple days ago and heard the nice guitar music coming through the window," she said. "That's all. Sorry."

As she turned to walk away Chris noticed how attractive she was and then said, "Wait, I'll be right out." He hurried outside and found himself excited for the first time since coming to Burton. He was pleased to find this cute girl still standing outside his window.

Chris found himself a little nervous as he tried to tell her, "You have a nice singing voice."

She looked into his eyes and said, "You're not from around here are you?"

Chris said, "No, that's for sure, and if I could go back to New York where I came from I'd be on the next bus. But I can't, so I won't, so I guess I'm here for a while the way it looks."

"I'm Jessie and I live across the street and down near the corner. I'm into music, like piano and voice at my school, so that's why your guitar playing caught my attention, that's all."

"I'm really glad to meet you and I guess I'm going to have to go to school in a week or so," said Chris. "Maybe we're in the same grade? I'm going to be a sophomore, how about you?"

Jessie quickly replied, "I'm going to be a junior this fall."

As small talk continued, an hour quickly passed by. Their conversations were about music and theater and other school activities. They thought that they would more than likely be in choir together.

Chris felt good about meeting Jessie, but found it strange that the first person he actually met in Burton was a girl. Jessie was a pretty girl but not the type that wore a lot of make up. She didn't need to because she had a natural glow to her face with penetrating blue eyes that captured Chris's attention right away. She had wisps of light sandy-colored hair that fell in front of her eyes and dimples that accented her beauty. She was a little tall for a girl, but seemed very comfortable with her height. The new friendship was off to a good start.

The next day Chris woke up feeling better about his new adventure in Burton, Iowa. Meeting Jessie helped to give him some optimism about his future in this little town. His mom even noticed a little change. He seemed to have a bounce in his step. She also noticed he was wearing cologne.

She said, "You sure smell nice this morning Chris. What's going on?"

Chris blushed and simply said, "Oh Mom!"

She then told him that they received a letter in the mail from the school about getting registered for classes. "We were asked to meet with the counselor and some teachers in order to get you signed up for classes this fall. They have it scheduled for next Wednesday afternoon."

He was wondering what kind of classes they have in a small school like this, besides Farming and Shop classes.

Chris finished his breakfast, quickly brushed his teeth and headed out the door, thinking he'd walk down the street and try to figure out where Jessie lived. As he walked down to the corner he thought he might be in the right neighborhood. He also began to feel uncomfortable and out of place again.

"Would she think I'm sorta strange just wandering by, as if she couldn't figure out what I'm up to?" he wondered.

Still unsure about where she lived, other things crossed Chris's mind, like maybe she had a big brother who would think he was stalking her, or worse yet, maybe she had a big boyfriend. Then he wondered how many other people might be watching him? Chris then paused and realized, how silly it was to feel so uncomfortable when he was only trying to find this new friend he just met.

As he walked by one house he thought he saw Jessie through the window. He caught a glimpse of her long hair hanging down behind the lacey curtains. He thought, "Should I wave at her from here or not? Did she see me?"

As he slowly walked to the door he decided to be brave and knock. Hoping it wasn't too early or meal time. Chris looked at his watch to find it was 9:50 a.m. As he knocked on the door he waited for a while and could hear someone running around inside. Finally the door opened and there was Jessie with a nervous smile.

She said "Hi Chris. How are you doing?"

He was still standing outside while Jessie was half hidden behind the door, almost as if she wasn't comfortable with having a guest.

Chris thought for a few seconds and said "I...I... want to ask you some questions about scheduling some classes at the school, that's all."

Jessie started to laugh and then came out from behind the door. She told Chris she was actually watching him through the window wandering around on the street but wasn't prepared for him to come to the door.

"I ran to put some things away and pick up some stuff. That's why I didn't answer the door right away. Please come in. So what's this about school that you were wondering?" Chris could smell some fresh minty toothpaste on her breath and a fresh fragrance of perfume.

Chris said "Well, that was just an excuse to try to find you I guess." Still very nervous, he grinned and said, "I was looking for your house and I guess I found it."

Jessie being a little nervous herself, quickly asked, "Did you bring your guitar with you?"

"No, I didn't," he replied.

Then Jessie took him by the hand and pulled him toward the piano in the living room. She told him to sit down and listen to a song. He sat on the edge of the bench as Jessie slid in from the other side. Chris suddenly realized he was sitting very close to a girl he just met yesterday. He wasn't sure what Jessie was feeling because she was older than him, and maybe she was just kind of playing with him, but nevertheless she certainly had his attention.

Jessie started playing a song by the Beatles." The song was "If I Fell". Chris was familiar with The Beatles music, so he enjoyed hearing Jessie sing the song. When Jessie went to the chorus, Chris found himself singing along. As soon as he found the melody Jessie went to a nice harmony above his voice, and it sounded so sweet! The words were on the sheet music, so they kept reading and singing as Jessie's pretty voice sang a nice harmony to him.

When they finished they both just said, "Wow!"

They sang again and again and they both had lots of fun. Burton, Iowa was becoming a little more tolerable. There was hope that just maybe things wouldn't be so bad.

The morning hours quickly flew by and soon it was lunch time, and time to say good-bye.

As Chris left, Jessie said in a soft voice, "Chris you're different from the boys around here. You like music and you're kind of bashful, and you have a tender heart. I can tell." She said, "I hope to see you again."

As he started walking away Jessie stretched out her neck a little and gave Chris a peck on the cheek. Chris was uncomfortable but flattered. His face turned a couple shades of red. When he left he felt like he floated up the street to his own house. He kept thinking about what Jessie said about him being different. As he got to the front door of his house he couldn't hide his emotions from his mother. She picked up on the smile and the joy on his face, and was happy to see that he wasn't so disappointed with their move. She made him a sandwich for lunch and they chatted about his morning walk.

Mike Murtha

Chapter Four

As the week went by he found himself calling Jessie almost every day. Twice that first week they got together to sing and play some music with the guitar and piano. The music and friendship made it easy for a hint of romance to surface a bit. Chris still wasn't sure where Jessie was coming from. Was it just friendship or more than that? He felt kind of funny being younger than Jessie and not sure where this friendship was going.

On Saturday Jessie called and asked Chris if he wanted to go somewhere in the car. Her folks let her take their car for a few hours. Chris's parents said it was okay so Jessie came over to pick him up. His dad commented how things had changed—the girls are picking up the boys! They commented that Jessie was a very nice girl and very good for Chris. She seemed confident, with musical talent, charm and good looks.

As the two of them drove around in Jessie's dad's car they listened to the radio and talked a lot. They both liked the same music. Some pop rock, some newer country and some of the oldies. They both were familiar with classical music. They decided to stop at the Dairy Queen over in the next town. The town was a little bigger than Burton. It was called Carlton, Iowa. "Home of the State Football Champs" the last two years. Carlton had been natural rivals with Burton every football season for the last forty years. When they pulled into the parking lot Chris noticed the same pickup truck that he admired at the baseball park earlier as he was exploring Burton.

He asked, "Jessie, who owns that pickup?"

She said, "That's Billy the Bully Snow's truck."

Chris just said "Oh," as he sank a little in the front seat of the car.

As they walked into the Dairy Queen, there he was. Billy spotted Chris across the room and said something nasty. Something like "Hey low life, what are you doing here?"

Before Chris could even say anything, Jessie quickly responded, "Hey Billy, shut your snuff-filled mouth. You don't even know this guy."

The rest of the group got a kick out of Jessie's quick wit and it made Billy feel a little dumb. This was okay for the moment but it didn't help to know that she was antagonizing Chris's newly formed enemy. Chris and Jessie hung around for a little while and had some malt shakes. Jessie introduced Chris to some of the other kids who happened to be from Burton. Chris was very grateful for Jessie's effort but at the same time it was uncomfortable getting acquainted.

Chris thought to himself later, "I don't remember anybody's name except Billy the Bully."

It was almost a week before school was to start when Chris met two other new friends. They were Cory and Mark. Jessie introduced them to Chris when they bumped into each other at the gas station. Cory was a friend of Jessie's through music. Chris found out lots of things about both Cory and Mark from Jessie. Cory played bass guitar and Jessie told Chris that he also had a nice voice. Cory seemed like a really nice guy who liked to laugh. He was fun to be around according to Jessie. He had a way of making people feel good. He was a naturally happy person. Cory also played on the football team. He was tall with brown hair that was cut short on the sides with a little wave on the top. Cory was slender but was fit and in good shape. He was a wide receiver and a defensive back on the football team. Cory was going into the 11th grade.

The other friend was Mark. His nickname was Elvis. Chris figured out Mark very quickly but Jessie had also filled Chris in on all the details about Mark. He was likable and a little crazy. He was very loud but basically harmless. Chris soon found out Mark already had two speeding tickets, one fender bender and had been kicked off the football team late last season for smoking and drinking at a party. Mark was going to be a senior but he seemed more like a person in his twenties. He even looked older. Chris also found out that he flunked Science class last spring. Mark was going to play football again this season but had to be held out for the first two games because of the failing grade in Science and the smoking and drinking violation from last season. He was a good football player because of his size. He was supposed to be the starting left tackle.

Chris found out that Mark was a huge Elvis fan. He even looked like Elvis. He combed his hair back like the early Elvis look. He had the black hair with sideburns. Mark was a very stocky and maybe he could be considered a little bit overweight. He had thick arms and legs. Music is what would soon bring Chris and Mark together. Jessie did a good job of giving her friends a little background on Chris as well. She explained to Cory and Mark that he was from New York and had a cool guitar. She certainly got a rise out of both Cory and Mark when she explained how they had been playing a little music together and how good Chris was at playing and singing. That was about all they had in common but that was enough to help start a good friendship.

Mark was a struggling sort of guitar player and would soon admire Chris's musical talents to be able to play the guitar as well as he did, and to sing so well. Mark hoped that Chris could help him learn more about music. Mark was more of a good listener of music and just liked to be around good music and fun.

It was Tuesday night and less than a week before school would be starting. Jessie invited Chris and Cory to come over to play some music. Cory brought his bass guitar, Chris had his six string acoustic guitar and they gathered around the piano with Jessie. Cory started playing a jazz bass line by himself and then Jessie found some cool chords that went together with Cory, then Chris came in with a really nice single string jazz solo. It was magic! All three of them became lost in the moment and after several minutes, still playing the same song they looked up and there was Elvis standing in the living room.

He said, "Sounds great guys!" Elvis never knocked, he just walked in. That was his style.

Jessie said, "Hey dummy, what are you doing here?"

Before Elvis could answer she scolded, "You've been smoking. I can smell it on you."

Elvis smirked and replied, "Don't always act like my mom. I hate it when you do that, Jess."

Elvis used to date one of Jessie's friends which was how they had become friends. As he listened to them play music the time just flew by. Cory sang some Eric Clapton songs, some old James Taylor songs and some pop standards. Chris was able to find some harmony to Cory's lead voice and Jessie found a high harmony. It was a good blend of musical instruments and some nice blending voices, but more importantly for Chris it was a good blend of some brand new friendships.

All of a sudden Cory said, "I've got to go, it's getting late. We've got football practice in the morning. That includes you too, Elvis."

Even though Elvis was being held out for the first two games, he was supposed to watch practice and attend team meetings. Cory commented how sore he was from football practice that morning. As everybody left, Chris once again thanked Jessie for making all of this happen, like introducing him to Cory and Elvis and getting to play some fun music.

As Chris was turning away he noticed a sparkle in Jessie's eye. He stopped for just a moment to look at her, and she gave him a big kiss right on his lips. He was caught by surprise and with a blushing smile said, "Wow, I didn't see that coming."

Jessie told him to go on home but to call her tomorrow. Jessie kind of slid across the floor to escort Chris to the front door. Chris glided home with his guitar in his hand. It seemed the stars were brighter and the air was fresher than ever. Then he realized he could clearly see the stars twinkling in the sky. In New York he could never see the stars because of all the city lights.

The next day Elvis somehow found Chris's home, and asked Chris if he wanted to go with him to watch football practice. Elvis was not able to practice yet because of his suspension but was expected to at least keep up with the team's practice from the sidelines. Chris agreed to go with him.

As they walked over to the field some of the guys yelled to Mark, "Hey Elvis, what's going on?" Even the coach called him Elvis.

Chris stood quietly on the side lines minding his own business when Billy Snow spotted him and said, "Hey sissy boy, why don't you come out for football."

Billy then threw a football as hard as he could at Chris. To his surprise, Chris caught it! At that moment everybody got real quiet. Chris, standing there holding the football with nothing to say, quickly found it lifted from his hands by Elvis. Then Elvis threw the ball back at Billy Snow's face. He threw it so hard that Billy did not have time to react and it bounced off of his face mask and hit the ground.

Elvis then yelled out to Billy, "You jerk, Snow. Take it easy."

The rest of the team witnessed most of this and started laughing. The only one that wasn't laughing was the coach, Mr. Smith. He was also the Phys. Ed. teacher.

He said, "Alright people, let's move on," and looking at Chris said, "Unless you are a part of this football team you better get going."

Chris and Elvis started walking away when the coach called out, "Hey Elvis, you better stick around. You just might learn something."

Chris quickly said, "See you Elvis," and walked home by himself.

As the rest of the week went by, Chris thought about what happened at the practice field and realized how much of a stranger he still was in this small town. The fear about going to school was increasing. Chris was again thinking how much he missed New York. In New York you didn't have to play football to fit in. Chris never had a chance to play sports in New York because there were so many kids, and trying to compete for a roster spot seemed far out of reach. The only competing Chris ever did with athletics was racing on foot with his old friend Joe on their way home from school, and apparently Joe wasn't much competition because Chris always won. Also Chris was more interested in music and theater. It seemed that in Iowa, the local football team was the only activity that mattered to anybody. That left Chris feeling a little uneasy.

Chapter Five

The first day of school was hard for Chris. Cory, the bass player friend called him early in the morning and offered to walk to school with Chris. Jessie had her circle of friends to hang out with and to kick off the new school year as well. She asked Cory if he could help Chris get off on the right foot. When they arrived at school there was a lot of parking lot activity, which didn't surprise Chris. Kids were listening to the radios in their cars and pickups. Some of the FFA guys were chewing snuff, and some flirting was going on between the boys and girls. Cory walked Chris over to one of the groups and quickly introduced him to some of the kids. Chris tried to remember some of the names. He had a good feeling about meeting the new kids only because of Cory, who apparently was a popular guy.

His mother had given him good advice before leaving home for school. She told him "Don't over dress or under dress. Don't make any big statements, smile a lot, and don't criticize anything or anybody, even if you don't agree with some of the things you see or hear."

Chris found his class schedule and he was very dependent on Cory to show him around the school. The school was an older three story brick building but was in good condition. Chris recalled his school in New York being the state of the art in design and it was equipped with all the latest and greatest of everything. His new school in Iowa was old but nice, it had open marble stairways and hardwood floors, and lockers lined the hallways. It had the smell of fresh paint and newly waxed floors, but also the fragrance of an old building. It was the old auditorium that really caught Chris's attention. It had a large stage with a beautiful dark blue velvet curtain that wrapped around the back and the front of the stage. It had a balcony high up from the main floor. As Chris walked through the auditorium he stopped and sang about six or eight notes of a melody and ended with a nice vibrato that echoed in the large area. He said out loud, "What a great sound!"

As luck would have it, the choir director, Ms. Oman happened to come out to the edge of the stage. She was a young looking, very attractive woman with light colored hair. She said, "Wow, I can spot a trained voice anywhere and that, my good man, is a very nice trained voice you have there. Come here," she said to Chris. As he walked toward the stage area she reached down with her hand and introduced herself.

"I'm Trisha Oman. What's your name?"

"I'm Chris Williams. I just moved here from New York City." Chris, being very nervous, looked up at Ms. Oman, now sitting down on the edge of the piano bench. She had a beautiful smile, wearing a red skirt that was slightly above her knees. As Chris looked upward from the floor while she was on the stage he couldn't help but to notice how attractive she was. She was swinging her shoe on her right foot by her toes. Chris started to feel a little uncomfortable and silly.

He quickly turned away as she said, "I hope you're planning on being in choir this year."

Chris looked back at her. She had her chin in her hand and her elbow on her knee. He noticed how white her teeth were against her bright red lipstick.

He then looked at the schedule in his hand and said, "Yes I'm with you sixth hour according to this."

She gave a short laugh, and said with a friendly smile, "Ok, then I'll see you sixth hour, Chris."

As he slowly walked away he could feel his heart beating a little faster. He thought Ms. Oman seemed very nice, and it gave him something to look forward to.

Things went well the rest of the day only because of people like Cory, Elvis, Jessie and Ms. Oman. Chris didn't see Jessie until the sixth hour in choir. She was the student piano player for Ms. Oman. It was so nice to see Jessie.

Through those first few days choir went well because music was fun and easy for Chris, largely because of all of the music classes he had taken back in New York. Chris had taken private voice lessons along with dance and theater. Compared to all of that, choir seemed pretty easy and fun in Burton, Iowa. It didn't take long for the other kids and Ms. Oman to figure out that Chris was a standout in this class. The only problem with this though was the simple fact that in this small town, and in this school, sports were much bigger and more important than music.

Later in the week the first class of the day was gym with Mr. Smith. Chris found out that this school mixed in the grades for Phys. Ed.. Some of the upperclassmen would be with the lower classes. Chris was glad to see Cory was in this group. Mr. Smith was the same Mr. Smith that coached football. He remembered Chris from being with Elvis on the sidelines at the football practice.

Mr. Smith said to Chris, "I read through your school records to find out that you are from New York City, and that you never played any sports. How come, boy?" he asked.

Chris was nervous but also a little upset that the teacher would single him out and put him on the hot seat.

Chris answered back, "Well sir, in spite of what you think, our family doesn't think the sun rises and sets on sports." The rest of the class giggled and went ooooh.

Mr. Smith didn't appreciate the answer or Chris's tone of voice. He said, "Well Mr. New York, maybe you better realize that you're not in New York anymore, but I do appreciate your spunk there, New York."

Then he told Chris to give him fifty pushups. That kept him too busy to play any of the games the other students were playing for a while. After class Mr. Smith came over and talked to Chris and said he was sorry for reacting so quickly, but he had his reasons. He told Chris he had never taught a student from New York City and wanted to make sure Chris didn't come in to this small school thinking he was better than anyone else. The other reason he questioned Chris about not playing sports was because in a small school, every able-bodied student was needed on the sports teams in order to have enough bodies to complete a team.

The rest of the week flew by. Soon it was Friday morning. The school was decorated for Football Friday. That's what they called every Friday in Burton during the football season. Some of the stores up town had banners in their windows. The school was playing its first game of the season. It was a conference game against Monroe, Iowa. Monroe was a little smaller school about twenty miles away. Burton was favored for this game. They liked to open the season with games like this to kick off the season with a win, hopefully. Jessie stopped Chris in the hallway early in the morning and asked if he wanted to go to the game with her and some of her friends.

Chris said "I don't know yet if I'm going or not." She quickly reminded Chris about the dance after the game that was in the gym.

Phys. Ed. on Fridays always meant that the football team didn't have to participate in class. This made it a little easier for Chris to fit in with a game of flag football. Chris was put on defense to play as a safety or corner back. He was told to play real deep because it looked like that might be a harmless place to put him so he didn't get in the way, more or less. As the game played itself out Chris found himself totally out of the action, not because he wasn't interested in playing, but Mr. Smith kept most of the action away from him. Chris didn't really care except he thought it was pretty narrow-minded of the teacher to just assume that Chris didn't have any athletic ability. When the class had almost finished Mr. Smith told everybody to run three laps around the field and then they could go in. As Chris was running with a group of kids they all passed the group of football players who were allowed to watch but not play on Friday. Billy Snow just happened to be in that bunch as the runners passed by. Billy stepped out and gave a shove to Chris's shoulder. It was just enough to throw Chris off balance and he headed to the ground. Some of the guys laughed and some just got real quiet. Mr. Smith happened to see the end of this and became very angry.

He stopped everybody in their tracks and said to Chris, "Hey New York, on your feet!"

When Chris stood up he noticed he had cut his right hand when he hit the ground. Mr. Smith said, "Hey boy, what's going on here?" As Chris looked over the teacher's shoulder he could see Billy shaking his head and his fist and signaling, hush!

Chris said, "Well Mr. Smith, I guess I was day dreaming and fell down."

Nearly everyone laughed and then moved on. Everybody but Cory. He came over and told Chris not to let that jerk push him around. Cory said he was going to let Mr. Smith know what really happened.

Chris said, "No! I don't think it's a good time to do that right now. Somehow this will work itself out."

Later in the day Jessie noticed Chris had a cut and swollen hand during choir. She was concerned but Chris just let it go. She could also tell that he just wasn't himself at all. Chris told Jessie he might just stay home on Friday night. She was a little disappointed but didn't question him.

That Friday evening Chris stayed home and could hear the field announcer calling out the games' plays from his house. It was one of those warm still nights when the sound just carried through the open air. As Chris sat out on the front porch trying to play his guitar with one sore hand, he thought about how different his life had become. A little tear came down his face from the pain in his hand and the pain of longing for the way life used to be. He then heard footsteps behind him. It was his Dad. He asked Chris if he was okay.

"I don't know what I am. Maybe a big baby or maybe a misfit."

Just then you could hear the P.A. announcer excitedly shouting "Another touchdown run by Billy Snow making the score twenty to zero, in favor of Burton!"

Chris said, "I think I know how that Monroe team feels right now."

Ben sat down and said to him, "I know how you feel. This isn't easy for me either but we've got to be strong. I don't know what's going on, Chris, but if there's a bully out there you cannot let him push you around."

Chris asked his dad how he knew about the bully thing. Ben said, "I just know, that's all. I want you to tell me all about it."

As Chris told the story about being pushed down in gym class he backed up the story with all the other little harassing moments that had happened and the problems he had with Billy Snow. Chris felt better talking to his dad about all of this. He thought his dad was a great listener, but he didn't really have a sure-fire cure for the problem.

He just told Chris, "Be yourself and be proud of that." He also said, "Don't give out any crap and don't take any crap!"

Chapter Six

The next day Cory and Jessie came over to see Chris. They decided to have a little fun with music. Cory had just bought a new Fender bass guitar and wanted to try it out. The three decided to meet at Jessie's house Saturday evening. Chris brought his Fender Strat electric guitar and a small P.A. system with a couple of microphones. Chris's mom helped him by driving over with the band equipment. This gave her a chance to meet Jessie's folks. As they were hooking up things for the P.A., the guitar amp and keyboard, Cory arrived with his bass amp and microphone. This made for a full room of band equipment, chords strung all over the place, not to mention the guitar cases. Jessie plugged her keyboard into an open channel on the P.A.

board. Jessie's mom just laughed at all the mess. She was very nice, a real free spirit, kind of an older hippy type.

As the three began playing and singing Chris's mom started smiling and couldn't believe how easy it seemed for the three of them to play music together. Chris himself was even impressed with how good it sounded. As they finished a little blues riff, Chris kicked off the intro to "Johnny B. Goode". The other two soon followed behind as Chris started singing the words. With the house vibrating from the music, all of a sudden Elvis came through the front door doing the Chuck Berry duck walk perfectly! Behind him trailed three or four other young kids, although not quite making the entrance that Elvis did.

After the song finished Elvis came over to Chris and said, "Wow man, that was great!"

Shaking Chris's hand just a little too aggressively, he let out a yell, "Ouch! My hand is cut and a little sore there Elvis."

Chris's mom, Cindy got a big kick out of Elvis and actually took the time to introduce herself. She noticed he looked old for his age and also noticed that he might have had beer on his breath. Not wanting to be a party pooper, Cindy didn't want to say anything to wreck the mood. She simply enjoyed watching Elvis enjoying the music so much. Soon after a little pause, Cindy decided to go home. She told Chris not be too late because they were planning to go to church in the morning. This was something they always did as a family back in New York. They were invited to the Lutheran Church by some people that worked with Chris's dad. It was a start for his parents making some new friends too.

As Sunday rolled around Chris's hand felt better. Playing guitar the night before was actually good for his hand and also good for the spirit, having fun with some friends. The church service went well for everybody in the family. The rest of the day was pretty laid back. They had a nice dinner and Chris took a walk around town. The one thing that kept going through Chris's mind was what his dad said about, 'don't give any crap to anybody and don't take any crap from anybody. ' The thought of standing up to Billy Snow was a little scary but he thought it might be time to do something. As Chris prepared for another week of school he thought his approach would be a little more aggressive in terms of dealing with Billy.

Chapter Seven

Monday started off and the first person Chris saw at school was ole' Elvis. Elvis said, "Chris, I love your music, man. You were really cook'n Saturday night." He then asked, "Do you think your mom could tell I'd been drinking? I sure hope not because I get to start playing football next week so I hope nothing happens to wreck that."

Chris looked at Elvis and said, "I don't think my mom really cares if you get to play football or drink beer or whatever. Elvis, you're a little crazy and that's why I like you!"

Elvis looked back at Chris and said, "Hey we're buddies and don't ever forget that, and if you ever need my help for anything just let me know."

That felt good to Chris and helped to start out the second week of school.

He did overhear his mom tell his dad that this Elvis kid smelled like alcohol and cigarettes. Not that she approved, but if that's all they're doing in Iowa, it wasn't so bad compared to the drug use by some teens in New York. Ben said that this was more like what kids did when they were young.

When Phys. Ed. class began that day Mr. Smith asked the kids to break up into groups of five. As the groups were quickly put together they found out they each would be running wind sprints in the gym. Wind sprints meant they had to line up on one end and run to the free throw line and back to the beginning, then run to the center line and back, and once again to the next free throw line and back, and then the full length of the gym and back. As the groups were put together Chris was glad to see Cory was in his group. Being on the football team, Cory was in good shape for this sort of drill. Both Cory and Chris watched the other groups, knowing their turn was coming up. Each group had a winner and they were told the five winners would compete to see who was the fastest kid in the class.

As the first group finished both Cory and Chris were not surprised that Billy Snow won in his group. Billy was actually a good athlete and for his size he could move pretty fast. Something different about being in a small school was that the gym class combined some boys from the upper and lower grades. It made it a little hard for the lower class members, but it was a way for the school not to have to hire two gym teachers and save some money. Finally Chris, Cory, and three others got to line up to run the drill. As Chris lined up he was thinking how fun it would be to do well at this. He remembered all the races he had back in New York with his friend Joe. He thought if he did well maybe Mr. Smith would treat him better and maybe Billy would lay off a little.

They got ready to go, Cory looked over at Chris and said, "Just stay with me tiger, give it all you got." As Mr. Smith barked off the commands to start the race Chris leaned way down low and wiped the dust off the bottom of his shoes just like Cory did. When they started running Chris kept thinking 'just stay with Cory, just stay with Cory.' After the first pivot Chris noticed he was a step or two ahead of Cory. As they ran the next stretch he noticed once again he gained a little more on Cory. Chris just kept thinking about staying ahead of Cory. As the sprints kept getting more stretched out Chris noticed he was gaining more distance on Cory. Then Chris was going all out on the last full length and he gave it all he had and realized he was blazing with speed that was almost out of control. Maybe it was the frustration with Billy Snow or the chance to show Mr. Smith he was more than just an odd kid from New

York. No matter what it was, Chris found himself running as if he was angry!

Soon the race was over and when Chris finished he noticed everybody else was at least five or six steps behind him.

Cory came over as he was trying to catch his breath and said to Chris, "Did you know you were that fast? My God, man, you're like super quick! Like world class speed!"

Chris said, "Cory, did you let me win?"

"No, I swear!"

Mr. Smith walked over to Chris and said, "Why didn't you tell me you were that fast kid? I'm impressed, let's see how you do in the finals there, Mr. New York."

They lined up the final five runners. Chris thought to himself for just a second, "Now I'm one of the elite runners in this class, and for now that feels pretty good."

Chris was still puffing from the first race and thought it wasn't fair to have to run so soon again, but it was only Phys. Ed., not the Olympics. As they lined up to race, wouldn't you know, Billy Snow happened to be right next to Chris. Much to his surprise Billy never said a word. Mr. Smith barked out the commands—'ready, set, go'—and the race began. Chris got a quick start and a one-step lead on Billy right away. As they would pivot and go back to the starting line, each time Chris gained another step or two on Billy. The next portion of the drill was the same in that Chris just kept gaining a step or two on everybody. On the last full length sprint of the full gym, Chris was just smoking, gaining speed the longer he ran. When he finished at the end of the gym, Chris stood there for a moment and realized he had beaten everybody by at least six or eight steps.

Going down on one knee to get his breath, soon Mr. Smith was right there to say, "Are you okay kid?" He then said, "You're something very, very special! Do you know that?"

As Chris lifted his head up he looked away from Mr. Smith and looked right at Billy Snow with confidence. Chris wanted to say something to Billy to rub it in a little, but he restrained himself from saying anything. He just stared at Billy while Billy dropped his head, shrugged his shoulders and slowly walked away. Chris then again thought about all the foot races he had with his old friend Joe back in New York.

Mr. Smith looked at his watch and under his breath said to himself, "Yes we've got time." He then said, "Everybody grab your sweatshirts, we're going outside."

Chris and the rest of the class wondered what was going on as they all dug through their lockers looking for a sweatshirt. As they filed outside they realized it was a cool and damp morning and the long sleeved shirts felt good. Mr. Smith told everybody to head over to the football field which was across the road from the school grounds. They were still uncertain of what was going on but nobody ever questioned Mr. Smith. As the class got to the one end of the football field they were told to all line up across the end zone area and prepare for an all-out foot race to the other end of the field.

Cory looked over at Chris and said, "I have a feeling this might have something to do with you, Mr. New York."

Mr. Smith then told everybody, "I want you to run full speed to the other end and we will start when I blow the whistle."

Again Cory looked at Chris and said, "Give it all ya got boy."

When the race began about five or six guys jumped out front right away. Billy and Cory were right there with them as Chris was keeping up. Mr. Smith positioned himself about halfway down the field and kept running ahead of the class as he looked back with a whistle in his mouth. As the group got to about the thirty five yard line Chris clearly found himself ahead of the pack by several steps. At midfield Chris was a good five to ten yards ahead of everybody. The class was in about three different groups by then. The slower group of about eight guys were in the rear, most of the class was in the middle, and out front was Cory, then Billy and clearly ahead of everybody was Chris. When they all reached the end of the field it was absolutely amazing how Chris had clearly out-run everybody. He finished a good ten to fifteen yards ahead of Cory and just behind Cory was Billy Snow. Mr. Smith conducted one more race to the other end of the field again and when that race was completed Chris was clearly the fastest runner in the whole group. Chris found this sort of funny because the football players should certainly be in better shape than he was. A few guys from the class came up to Chris and made some comments about his blazing speed.

Cory was still puffing and said, "Wow Chris, you made us all look like we were standing still!"

After class Mr. Smith said "Chris, I need to talk to you boy. I want to talk to you about playing football."

Mr. Smith explained to Chris how impressed he was with his ability to run with such quickness in his step.

He said to Chris, "Please take me very serious. I'm very honest when I say you have been blessed with a very special God-given talent. Go home and talk it over with your parents and hopefully they will give you permission to play football."

He handed Chris a card to get a physical and told him, "Go see the doctor and get this filled out, and please consider coming to football practice as soon as you can."

Chris thought for a second and said, "I never got to play football before, but I always followed the Jets in New York. I just don't know what I could do on the team to fit in?"

Mr. Smith said, "Chris you have speed and quickness like I haven't witnessed in years. That kind of speed is a gift. With the sort of quickness I saw you display, I know we can find a place for you on this team. There's always a place for speedy guys on a football team and you, Mr. New York, are a very speedy guy."

Chris honestly did not know he had a special talent to run faster than most kids his age other than Joe. He was never tested and never aware of his special gift.

Chris looked at the physical card and said, "Mr. Smith, I'll think about it and let you know. "

As Chris walked away he had a lighter step to his walk and the rest of his day went really well. Before this, the only thing that meant anything to him was music and the arts. That evening Chris told his folks what happened. After telling all the details about the races that went on in Phys. Ed. class, Chris's dad recalled a story about a great uncle that set a college track record many years ago. He thought it was in the one hundred yard dash at Princeton University. Ben shared the story with Chris and Cindy how this uncle held the school record for nearly ten years.

"It must be in your blood Chris, " said Ben.

Much to Chris's surprise both of his parents were very supportive. Chris thought about what happened. It was as much of a surprise to him as it was to the football coach, Mr. Smith, Cory, the whole class and especially to Billy Snow. Chris had never competed in sports before and never knew that he might have a special talent. His only worry was whether or not he had talent worth all the high expectations of Mr. Smith.

"Can I really contribute something to the football team?" he wondered.

Chapter Eight

The next day Chris's mom made an appointment for a physical exam at the local clinic. Everything was good and the doctor signed the physical card. Wednesday morning Chris went to school and talked to the coach about joining the team. As Chris walked into Mr. Smith's office he was greeted with a handsome smile from the coach.

"Well, New York," he said, "Are you here to tell me some good news?"

Chris thought how much different he was being treated now compared to the first day of school by the coach.

Chris said, "Well Mr. Smith, I would like to join the team."

The coach smiled and simply said, "See you after school in the locker room and we'll fit you with some pads and a helmet."

During the whole school day it became very hard for Chris to think about anything but football practice. He just couldn't believe it himself that he was going to get a chance to learn how to play football with a real, organized team. After arriving at the locker room and getting introduced to a few guys by Cory, Chris was told to weigh in and measure his height. His weight was 168 pounds and he was 5'10". It was steamy from all the showers, and the smell of wet towels. Chris then got his pads, helmet and a practice jersey. He was handed a pair of football shoes by the team manager when Mr. Smith walked in and intervened.

He told the manager, "Give this kid some light weight low tops, not a lineman's high top shoes."

Most players bought their own shoes, to their liking. For now Chris had to wear the school's assigned shoes. As Chris walked out the door and on to the practice field, the first person that came up to him was Elvis. He mentioned that he was in the same boat as Chris because he was just getting started as well because of his suspension.

Elvis hollered, "Hey buddy, this will be great having you here!" Elvis was talking so close to him that their face masks actually hit. Chris could smell cigarettes on Elvis's breath and thought, this guy is a wild man, or a little bit crazy. Chris also noticed he felt a little taller standing on the hard ground with spiked shoes.

From what Chris was told the practice was routine. They started out with lots of stretches and exercises to get prepared for actual football contact. After finishing the normal drills everybody split up into their groups of offense and defense. Chris looked around wondering where he should go. Feeling a little uneasy, he soon found Mr. Smith and was told to report with the punter and help retrieve balls. Chris found the area where the kickers were practicing and figured out what was going on. The kickers spread out about forty yards apart and just kicked the ball back and forth.

Coach Smith told Chris, "I simply want you to catch the ball and hand it to the other kicker. He will kick it back and so on and so on."

As the punters moved into position, Chris found himself down field ready to catch the ball. As the first ball flew high in the air Chris was fighting with the sun to see it and tried to adjust, but looking into the sun and not ever having experienced looking around a face mask made things challenging. The cleats in his football shoes dug in more than Chris expected when he started to run towards the ball. It caused him to stumble. As he attempted to catch the first ball, he soon realized he over-reacted to the kick and was way too close to catch the ball. It went sailing way over his head. The kickers never stopped their routine. They just kept kicking footballs, one after another.

Before long Chris was catching about three out of four footballs that were kicked at him. This drill went on for about thirty minutes. After that Chris was put into the tackling and blocking drills. Then everybody had to do some running around the field. Finally the practice was over and not too soon for Chris. After the showers he found himself very tired and a little sore.

At supper both of his parents noticed how exhausted Chris looked. The next day walking to school Chris found himself limping just a bit. He remembered that through the night he had leg cramps which woke him up a couple times. While he walked down the street he noticed a car slowing down behind him, and then pulled up alongside him. As the rider's window rolled down Chris quickly saw that it was Ms. Oman. When she leaned over to talk to him, he noticed her wide smile and bright white teeth.

She said, "Chris, hop in and I'll give you a ride to school."

Chris, being a little shy said, "Well, okay I guess, because my legs are a little sore today. I just had my first football practice last night and I'm not feeling too sharp today."

Before she responded Chris thought how nice her perfume smelled, especially being in that enclosed area.

She then said, "You just looked like you needed a ride. The real reason I stopped is to ask you Chris, if you would consider singing a solo at our fall concert?"

As she turned the corner into the school parking lot her coffee cup began to tip over and Chris grabbed it quickly and kept it from spilling. Another big smile came across her face and those bright white teeth were exposed once again.

She said, "Oh thank you. That would've stained my new dress. Chris, you're a life saver!"

Ms. Oman parked her car in the parking lot and again asked him if he would show off some of that New York talent and consider singing a solo at the concert.

Chris said, "Well, I just started football and my classes are keeping me busy, I'm just not sure of anything right now."

While they walked from the car to the front door of the school she said, "Please give it some thought and I'll see you later in choir."

As she walked away Chris was caught up in thinking about her offer to have him sing a solo at the concert and almost forgot to say thank you for the ride to school. As he thanked her she didn't turn around, she just put her hand up over her shoulder and sort of waved back at Chris. Her high heeled shoes clicked as she swayed down the hallway. Chris wondered if Ms. Oman was using her good looks in a way to persuade him to do some special music. Her little gestures of flirting really meant nothing. It was only a way to get Chris's attention and get him to do some special things in choir for her. He realized it was her way of manipulating him a little, but Chris still enjoyed the attention.

That night at practice Chris was again put to the test with the punters. As they kept kicking the footballs at a steady pace Chris just kept catching them one after another after another.

There was very little talking between the kickers until one punter walked over to Chris and said, "Hey, they call me Spider Wilson. I'm the Spider Man! I thought I should tell you my name if we're going to play together." Spider was black and maybe the only black kid in this little town.

Spider said, "I already know your name, Chris. Do you know what they're planning on doing with you on the team?"

Chris replied, "Not really."

Spider, who was also a defensive back and a wide receiver said, "Maybe you're going to be the punt and kick-off returner."

At first Chris felt a little fear thinking of doing that and then quickly said, "Wow, Spider, I hope you're right about that. "

As the practice came to a close Chris again found himself very exhausted and worn out. The coach came over to Chris and asked him if he could meet with him that night at the field around 8:00.

He thought for a second and quickly said, "Sure Mr. Smith, whatever."

That night the punter, Spider, Coach and Chris went to the playing field and set up for the same kind of routine of practicing catching the football. The field was lighted on only one end of the field. The grass looked so green in the light, while the night sky was growing darker. The coach began giving instructions.

He said, "Chris, I'll be honest with you. This is a test I do to see if a player has the instinct to play this position. I will have Spider kick the ball from the dark end of the field. He will kick it to you into the lights and we'll see if you can react to the ball."

The coach then said, "All that speed you have doesn't do us much good if you can't catch the ball. It's a simple way for me to see if you have what it takes to play this position of returning kicks in a game. I'll know in about four kicks if you are any good at this."

Chris thought, "boy they sure take their football serious around here." Chris strapped on his helmet and was ready to go. He soon realized he really could not see the punter on the dark side of the field. Chris thought maybe he would be able to hear the ball being kicked and would be able to react to the kick that way. Just then Coach Smith turned on the P.A. system and had crowd noise recorded, and turned it up very loud. At that time Chris could feel his knee's getting a little shaky and then just like that, there came the first football flying through the sky. Chris remembered not to make the same mistake of running towards the ball too soon. As he sighted in the angle of the ball he kept his eyes on the football until it was in his grasp. He cradled it like a baby for just a moment as he gave a sigh of relief.

All of a sudden another football was flying through the sky, so Chris quickly dropped the one in his hands and tried to react to the next ball. Again the noise and chaos was a bit overwhelming as he adjusted to the ball but again, caught the second football. The volume of the P.A. slowly was being lowered as another ball came flying through the air. This time Chris had to side step to make the catch. In the process he found himself stumbling and tumbling forward over one of the footballs that he had tossed on the ground. Just before he fell to the ground he caught the ball that had been sailing through the air. As he landed on the ground he squeezed the ball tightly to his chest. As Chris lay on the ground he could hear both Coach Smith and the punter, Spider laughing.

"Hey New York," said Coach Smith, "You did pretty good! You passed the test. Way to go kid!"

When they walked back into the school the coach told Chris he wanted him to watch some film and try to learn some more about his job on special teams. They spent some time watching blocking schemes for kick-off and punt returns. It was now nearly 10:00 and Chris was very tired and ready to go home.

Mike Murtha

Chapter Nine

The next day was Football Friday which was also game day. The school was decorated with football cut outs on the walls of the hallways, with crepe paper streamers and large banners everywhere. The varsity players all wore their jerseys with their jeans. It made them feel very special. Chris was issued jersey number twenty-three. However he was told he would not be eligible to play yet because of a lack of practices according to the conference rules.

When Jessie saw Chris wearing a football jersey she smiled and said, "Wow, you look pretty handsome in that cool shirt!" Jessie asked Chris if he wanted to go somewhere after the game.

Chris said, "Sure, I'm supposed to sit on the bench with the team tonight, but right after the game let's get together."

As Chris was leaving school he found himself being followed out the door. He stopped to look and was surprised to find it was Ms. Oman.

She said, "Chris, have you found any time for music this week?"

"Oh, Ms. Oman, I'm sorry I couldn't make choir today because we had a football meeting and I think we were all given permission to attend our meeting."

She replied, "Chris, you told me you joined the football team and good for you, but don't overlook the special things in our school like music and the arts. You know this stuff. You were brought up in it. Football is such a big deal in this small town but real talent and joy come from expressing music, in my opinion. You have some special talents in those areas, please don't ignore that."

"Thank you Ms. Oman, I've always put music and drama and all the arts at the top of my list, but I discovered I might have a talent in athletics too. I just might, I don't know for sure, but I just might," he said.

"OK Chris," she said, "I'll forgive you this time if you will promise to sing a solo at the fall concert."

He said, "Well I don't have much time to prepare 'cause I've got football practice and all of that, but I will think about it."

As he looked at that persuasive smile from Ms. Oman and her pretty face projecting a twinkle in her eye, her arms folded in a way that spoke a body language very hard to ignore.

Chris felt trapped, and softly said "Well, yes I'll do something."

Ms. Oman quickly approached him, patted him on the shoulder and said, "Thanks, Chris!"

As she started to walk away Chris was caught up in watching her sway as she walked and then he suddenly said, "Ms. Oman, could I put something together with Jessie and Cory?"

She quickly turned around and said, "Well yes, now you're talking like a creative musician again. Chris, that will work if you show me what you can come up with real soon."

As she walked to the parking lot Chris watched her again. He knew that her little gestures were only a way for her to persuade him to do something special in choir for her.

As the players loaded the bus for Kellogg, Iowa to play football, Chris filed in line with Cory and Elvis. Cory was a smooth athlete with a quiet confidence about himself. Elvis was often outspoken, but very funny and maybe somewhat insecure. The three sat together and talked football and music. Chris had a chance to ask Cory if he would consider playing a song or two with him at the fall concert next week. He still needed to ask Jessie.

Cory said sure he would be glad to, "Whatever you need there, New York."

Elvis quickly spoke up and said, "Hey you guys, do ya need a drummer?"

Chris quickly thought "oh no, not you Elvis."

Then Elvis told the guys he had this nineteen-year old friend who was a pretty good drummer and he knew he'd like to play with them. Chris and Cory were both reluctant to answer but just about then Coach stood up and began talking about the game. It was hard for Elvis to focus on anything very long but soon he was all ears and eyes for Coach Smith.

As the players dressed for the game the tension built. After some last minute instructions the team filed out of the old locker room. When they ran onto the field the Burton Bulldogs were led by their captain Billy Snow. The Bulldogs won the opening toss and elected to go on offense first. Billy Snow was deep to accept the kick. Coach Smith made a point to get Chris up close to see the action so he could get a feel for what to expect. As the ball sailed through the air Chris thought, "Wow, I've already got butterflies."

Coach quickly made a comment to Chris about waiting for the wedge to form and then watch for your lanes to open. Billy took the ball and tucked it under his arm as he started up field. Billy was sort of fast for being a big guy and had power and a lot of guts. As he attempted to run up field he was outrun by the defenders and was soon tackled. The game went back and forth with very little offense. In the first half the Burton Bulldogs intercepted a pass that really looked more like a wounded duck. This set up a late drive that resulted in a seven to zero score at halftime.

At the half Chris stood out of the way but within listening range to hear Coach Smith attempt to rally the team. When the second half began Burton soon took control and never looked back. Cory had one interception with a return that nearly took him to the end zone. Three plays later Burton scored an easy touchdown with a soft pass from senior quarterback Joey Hamilton to none other than Billy Snow. The final score was twenty-seven to six, Burton winning very handily.

Chris said to Cory and Elvis on the way home, "Man, I feel a little out of place. You guys don't need me. Why does the Coach want me to be a part of this?"

Elvis said, "It's a team sport. Just bring what ya got and go all out. If we all do that, we will always do well. It'll be fun to see you outrun some of the defenders next week there, New York. Now where's the party tonight?"

Jessie was waiting for Chris at the school with a big smile and a big Coke. She said, "Hey guys, way to go! We heard you won."

Chris quickly told Jessie about Cory's interception and how it helped to put the game away. Chris said, "He was just great!"

Cory put Chris in a head lock and said, "Shut up squirt, it was nothing. I hope I can get a few more of those this season."

The three of them got in Jessie's mom's car and drove to the local café where everybody met after the games. Soon after they arrived Elvis walked in with some girl he knew from another town. She looked older and probably was no longer in school. She had a lot of makeup on and a lot of perfume. As Elvis walked over to introduce her they could smell the cigarette smoke on both of them. While Elvis talked and laughed Chris realized he was finally getting comfortable with some pretty good friends. Chris had a chance to talk to everybody about the plans for the upcoming fall concert next week.

Chapter Ten

Saturday morning rolled around and Cory, Jessie, and Chris started making plans for a practice. They decided to set up that night in the garage at Jessie's home. With the intentions of just practicing, they thought it might be fun to invite a few friends over. It wasn't long after they were getting plans pulled together when the phone rang. It was Elvis wanting to get together with everybody that same night. They filled Elvis in on the little party and he quickly responded he would be there with his drummer friend also. The plans were made and soon it was early Saturday evening.

It was a nice, warm fall night. The sky was clear and the crescent moon was just rising. They began by setting up the P.A. and amps along with the portable piano for Jessie. She got the piano for Christmas last year. When they plugged it into the P.A. directly it sounded really good. Cory rolled in his amp and had it set up and plugged in. Chris was trying to get things pulled together for himself when over his shoulder he heard Elvis talking loudly while he was asking everyone to meet his drummer friend Karl. As he introduced Karl to everybody, Chris took notice of his longer dark hair and a John Deere cap pulled down near his eyes. He was quite tall with about a three-day beard.

Chris quickly stuck out his hand and said, "Nice to meet you Karl. If you got your drums along it's okay with me to have you sit in."

Karl spoke in a deep low voice. It didn't take long for Cory and Jessie to get acquainted with Karl. He started setting up his drums and they talked a little about the tunes they knew. He seemed to be at ease with the whole thing.

Elvis said, "Chris, if this thing works out with you guys and Karl, you're going to owe me big time."

Chris asked, "Like what Elvis?"

He said, "Let me sing a song with you."

Chris raised his eyebrows but didn't answer him.

Soon after they were all set up, the music started with some old time rock 'n' roll. They played some easy songs for Karl to follow along. A number of people showed up as the party began and the music flowed naturally. Chris and

Jessie sang most of the songs and Cory did some nice harmony but also sang lead on a few songs as well. What they quickly discovered was that Karl was good. What was really cool was his low voice singing along with them and finding some great low harmonies to their songs. As the night went along they became more and more comfortable blending the instruments and voices. Karl even took a solo on the drums. At one break they set up a microphone for Karl's voice and things just seemed to flow with a fun blend of harmonies. The crowd of kids along with Jessie's mom and Chris's parents had a great time. Chris had a natural feel for playing lead guitar, and used a little distortion on his amp. He had great tone for playing nice leads. It all fit so nice.

As the evening wound down Chris took the time to talk to everyone about playing a couple songs at the fall school concert. After some discussion they all agreed on the song selection. Even Karl was willing to come and play if the school would allow it. Karl worked at the local Feed Mill and also part time for a farmer in the area. He said he thought he could change his schedule if they wanted him to play. Finally everybody left except Jessie and Chris. Jessie put her arm around Chris and gave him a soft kiss on the cheek.

She said, "I don't know if you noticed but some of the cheerleaders were here tonight and they were sure giving you the eye." Then she said, "I'm just a little jealous."

Chris had a blank look on his face.

Jessie said, "I don't think you notice much around you sometimes Chris. Like me!"

With a silly grin he said, "Don't think for one minute I don't notice you or think about you a lot." He then said, "I can feel myself blushing every time I'm around you."

She said, "You sure don't act bashful when you sing or play your guitar."

Chris replied, "That's easy for me. Girl stuff isn't so easy for me."

As Chris was talking, not once did he look at Jessie in the face. She then took his chin and turned his head toward her and looked him in the eyes. Her blue eyes were penetrating.

She smiled and said, "Yes, I will be patient with you if you'll be aware of my feelings."

She then raised her eyebrows and placed a kiss on Chris's lips.

Chris blushed and said, "Wow, don't forget I'm a little younger than you and I'm just not too good at this."

Jessie said, "I know what you are and I like what I see. So there!"

Chapter Eleven

On Tuesday night the fall concert began in the old gymnasium, which had a stage on the one end. The choir sang five songs. This included Jessie and Chris. Jessie played the piano. The choir sounded really nice. There would be just a short break and then the school band would play. As the concert band started playing, Chris, Jessie and Cory got organized to play their two songs. Jessie did get permission to let Karl play and soon he and Elvis showed up hauling in the drums through the side door. They were quietly working so as not to disturb the concert band. They had not clearly decided what to do until Jessie suggested to start with a slow song by the Beatles. Then she thought they should do a good rocker. Karl spoke up and said, "I'm all for a good rocker!" They decided on "Sweet Home Alabama" for the second song.

The high school band was still playing. They were on the gym floor while Chris and the rest of the guys were on the stage with the curtains closed. Soon after the high school band finished up, Ms. Oman took the time to explain a little about the special music that was coming up next. As she explained where Chris was from and that he was new to their school this year, someone slowly opened the velvet curtains.

When they were just about all the way open Chris looked back at Karl and said, "Hey let's change things up and do the faster song first."

A big grin came across Karl's face and his whole face lit up as he clicked his sticks together four times and Chris kicked off the intro to "Sweet Home Alabama." Eight beats later the band was in high gear and so was most of the student body as they reacted with a lot of energy and applause. The high school principal was not enjoying the music as much as everybody else was. It was obvious because he had his hands covering his ears and shaking his head. Ms. Oman was grinning ear to ear and was bouncing to the music. She then gave a look of encouragement up at Chris as he was singing the lead vocal to the song. When Chris saw this, it gave him confidence and he began singing with a comfortable command. The parents in the crowd were a little unsure of what was going on at first, but soon got caught up in the moment along with the student body and began to sway and bounce with the music like everybody else. When the song ended the crowd responded with huge applause and cheers. The principal, Mr. White, looked over at them and gave them a slight nod and grin and then slowly clapped his hands together.

As soon as the song was over Chris looked over at Jessie and saw on her face a look of stage fright along with a look of excitement.

She looked to Chris for direction and he said, "OK, now let's do, 'If I Fell' by the Beatles."

As they started singing the song together, calmness came over Jessie. Their voices seemed to blend like magic and some of the crowd responded by smiling and swaying with their hands up in the air. When they finished the second song Chris, Jessie, Cory and Karl all looked at each other with sheer joy. The applause was so genuine from the audience. They felt as if they went to Heaven for just that short moment.

The wonderful mood quickly changed as a loud voice in the back of the gym let out a sarcastic "Yee Ha, you bunch of pansies."

It was Billy Snow. He was trying to ruin their fun. Most of the crowd turned around and looked at Billy. He got just what he wanted, the attention on him. Karl slammed his sticks down across the snare drum and stood up.

He said, "Who is that jerk? I want to shut him up right now."

Cory and Chris quickly grabbed him and said, "Cool it Karl, so we don't screw this up."

Karl had a tough time letting it go but he did cool off. As the group packed up their gear after the concert, they talked about how much fun it was to play and get that kind of a reaction from the audience, in spite of Billy Snow. They started making plans for playing again the next Saturday night.

Chapter Twelve

The rest of the week went by quickly between football practice and school work. Before they knew it, it was Friday night. The football team had a home game with the Spensor Wildcats. Spensor, Iowa was a good football community with a lot of support from the town folks. They always had a good following for their football teams. Chris was told that normally Spensor would fill the bleachers with their fans on the visitor's side. This night might be a little different because of a steady rain that started late afternoon and never quit. After they got dressed in their pads and uniforms they met in the gym for a quick meeting. Coach Smith met with each group starting with the offense, and then the defense as well as the special teams. He had a final word with the whole team to rally their spirits. Coach Smith had a talent for motivating people.

Chris was excited about playing his first game as a kick-off and punt returner until Coach Smith came over to Chris and said, "I'm a little leery about having you play tonight with this rain coming down so hard. I've decided to let Billy Snow return kicks and punts tonight."

At that point Chris felt let down and disappointed with Coach Smith's decision.

On the opening kick-off Billy caught the ball on the twenty-one yard line and returned it to the forty. As they watched Billy run, the mud flew off the bottom of his cleats. Because of the rain and the mud the game looked to be in slow motion. The Burton Bulldogs hung in there with very little offense and a lot of defense. At half time the Bulldogs led two to zero. The two points came off a fumbled snap by the Spensor Wildcats' quarterback. He recovered his own fumble, but it was in the end zone which resulted in a safety for the Burton Bulldogs.

At half time most of the players were wet and full of mud. All except for number twenty-three, which was Chris. Chris left his warm-up jacket on the whole first half and never took off his helmet. As the second half began Chris began to lose a little interest knowing he probably wasn't going to play, and the rain just kept coming down. Midway in the fourth quarter the Bulldogs' quarterback, Joey Hamilton ran a boot leg to the right and attempted to cut upfield when the ball popped out and landed in the arms of the outside linebacker for the Spensor Wildcats. He took two steps and was off and running. He ran right past the Bulldogs bench with a few would-be tacklers trailing behind him and wound up in the end zone for a Wildcats touchdown. Billy Snow might have had a chance to catch him because he had the best angle of any of the Burton Bulldogs but it looked like Billy sort of gave up.

The game ended with an ugly score of six to two in favor of the Wildcats from Spensor. As all the players filed into the locker room they were a sad rain-soaked bunch of guys. As for Chris, the only part of him that was wet was his feet. He never bothered to shower. Cory and especially Elvis came off the field totally soaked and full of mud. You couldn't even read number seventy-five on Elvis's jersey. This was one of the first times Elvis was pretty quiet around Chris. That didn't last long though. After Elvis showered and dressed and was out in the parking lot he started in joking around again. Cory came out of the locker room and said he didn't feel much like doing anything but promised to get together on Saturday night. As Cory walked away Chris couldn't help notice and admire Cory's confidence and his poise. Even after losing the game Cory could walk away with his head held high. Chris thought that he was really one of the cool guys of their school. He thought to himself how lucky he was to have a friend like Cory.

Then there was Elvis. As they were all walking across the parking lot Elvis was just talking the whole time even from a distance. Elvis asked Chris if he needed a ride home.

Chris replied "No thanks, my mom is on the way to pick me up."

Elvis said, "I'll call you tomorrow about the practice with Karl the drummer for Saturday night. I'm still thinking of a song to sing with you guys."

He reminded Chris that he had promised that he could sing a song with the band for finding a drummer for them. Chris wasn't sure where the promise to Elvis was going to take them but he thought, "Oh well." He watched Elvis drive off from the parking lot. It wasn't long before he could hear the stereo cranked up in volume and he could see him lighting up a cigarette. Chris laughed to himself and shook his head as he walked away.

Jessie had to babysit for her older sister's kids so she wasn't around after the game. As Chris walked away from the parking lot he saw his mother pull up to give him a ride home. She was wet and cold from watching the game. When Chris got into the car she asked if he was disappointed that he didn't get to play. Chris said he really didn't know how he felt yet because he hadn't played. He reminded his mom that he was only a sophomore and the other guys were upper classmen. He told his mother that he would get his chance.

Chris's mom then said, "Oh, I heard from your sister tonight. Vickie called after supper. She said she might be coming here to see us sometime this fall."

Chris thought with all the crazy changes in his life he really hadn't thought a whole lot about his sister in college.

He said, "Mom I feel kind of guilty because I haven't even thought about Vickie. How is she?"

She filled him in on Vickie and they talked about her all the way home. As Chris went to sleep that night he thought about the long run that resulted in a touchdown for the other team and how easily they scored. It seemed that no one on his team could catch him. Chris wondered that if he was given the chance, if he could've run that guy down?

Saturday afternoon Chris's dad came home from a business trip and wanted to hear all about the game. Chris told him that he didn't miss much.

"We lost and I didn't play," he said.

Saturday afternoon Chris started practicing some songs for that evening. They agreed to meet at Jessie's place again and set up in the garage. After going over some of the songs, Chris decided to go for a little run. As he walked and ran slowly through the streets he couldn't get over how quiet the small town was on a Saturday afternoon. Chris looked into some of the old store front windows and thought once again how much different life was here compared to New York. There was always noise and motion going on in

New York, and people all around. Chris wondered if he had to make a choice between Iowa or New York City right now, which would he choose.

Walking around town he took in all the calm and peacefulness of the small town. Chris started to break into a running pace again when he noticed a red car was following him. When Chris finally stopped and turned around it caught him off guard. The man behind the wheel was wearing a white collar. It turned out to be the minister from the local Lutheran church.

He said, "Excuse me son, but are you Chris?"

He replied, "Yes sir, I am. "

The minister then introduced himself as Pastor Jim from the First Lutheran Church of Christ. "The reason I stopped you is because I'm looking for some help to move the church organ."

Chris did remember him from going to some Sunday morning services with his parents but wasn't sure how the minister knew who he was.

"My helpers didn't show up like they said they would," said the minister. "Could you help me Chris?"

Chris thought he really couldn't say no to the minister. He jumped into the car and they headed off to the church. As they arrived there Chris realized how easy it was to talk with the pastor and thought how quickly they became friends. While they moved the organ the two of them kept the conversation going with some lively laughter and good stories. Pastor Jim asked Chris about his background, so Chris told him all about New York and how they ended up in Iowa. When the Pastor told his story it turned out to be a little bit like Chris's because Pastor Jim came from a large city as well. He grew up in Chicago and later married and ended up in Iowa.

As they shared their stories Chris told him about his music and about their practice that night to be held at Jessie's.

Pastor Jim tried not to start preaching to Chris, however he told him, "Go slow with your relationships and don't overlook the power you hold with music."

As they finished up Chris realized he had a pretty good time talking with the pastor. When Pastor Jim brought him back home he revealed that he was at the school the night Chris played at the fall concert.

He told Chris, "That's how I knew your name. You have a real talent for music."

He then asked Chris if he would ever consider playing in the church. He told him that they have a contemporary service every Sunday night.

Chris replied, "Well thanks for saying those nice things about my music, and I'll give some thought about doing some music at church."

As they parted the Pastor thanked Chris for the help. He then gave him his card with the church schedule on it and invited Chris and his family to be a part of the church anytime. Chris thought it was certainly a different afternoon, but it was sure a fun experience.

When Saturday night arrived it felt like a perfect evening. The fall air was still warm and the sky had cleared, the moon was just about full. As they started setting up the equipment some of the kids started to show up. It was fun to see the different cars some of the guys were driving. A few of the guys had their FFA jackets on and others had their letterman jackets on. The FFA guys were typically shop guys with grease under their finger nails. Their cars were their pride and joy. With all these people showing up it made Chris realize what Pastor Jim had said about the power of music. Elvis and Karl arrived and began setting up the drums in the back of the garage. Chris's folks popped in to hear a little music. Jessie's parents were just inside the breezeway. It was going to be fun, thought Chris, because they had put together just enough good songs to sound organized. Cory got there a little late but soon they were ready to start playing. Jessie wrote up a set sheet and the group went right down the list and everything flowed nicely. During their breaks Elvis and Karl spent a lot of time talking to all the girls. Jessie kept a close eye on Chris most of the night. She had a mother-like wisdom about her. Chris didn't mind. He realized how smart and mature she was for her age.

When the night came to an end they watched the cool cars drive off. As they packed up all the band equipment Chris's folks were talking to Jessie's parents and commented how nice it was that Jessie had helped Chris feel more acquainted with the other kids. They remarked that it was nice it was that they could play and sing so well together. Ben and Cindy were ready to leave and told Chris not to be too late. As his dad turned away Chris started cleaning up all the pop cans. He noticed a small empty bottle of Jack Daniels where Elvis and Karl were hanging out during the breaks. Chris shuffled the bottle under some old rags before his dad saw it. He didn't think his dad had seen it but he wasn't sure. At least Ben never let on. Chris began thinking about Elvis and Karl and then realized why they were so talkative with all the girls. Chris also hid the empty bottle from Jessie. She would be very angry if she knew about the drinking. All in all no harm done and everybody had a really good time. As Chris went to say good-bye to Jessie, he initiated the kiss for a change. It caught Jessie a little off guard. She responded with a nice, long hug. She told Chris how much life he brought to their little town. Again Chris thought about what the pastor told him about the power of music.

Sunday night Chris asked Jessie if she would go to church with him. As they arrived at church Pastor Jim welcomed them to the service. Chris thought the music was pretty cool. Some of it was recorded and a group of kids sang along to the music. Most of it was led by the pastor's wife who played the piano, and she also played an acoustic guitar on some songs.

Chapter Thirteen

Monday after school it was back to football practice where they found Coach Smith upset about their effort last Friday night. He reminded the whole team that the bad weather was no excuse for their poor effort. He said the Spensor football team didn't like playing in bad weather any better than they did. They just wanted to win more than we did. As they broke into their position groups one of the assistant coaches asked Chris to join in on the defense tackling drills. He asked Chris if he had ever played any defense. Chris told him no, he hadn't but would like to. Chris assured him he would be willing to learn if the coaches would help him. What the coaches had in mind was to prepare Chris to play on some special teams if they felt they needed him and at deep safety.

The coaches told him "No promises, but we need you to be prepared in case we have some injuries to our starting group."

Coach Smith said, "Chris, last Friday night when we gave up that long run that lost the game for us, we think you could've caught that runner and prevented him from scoring their touchdown."

Chris wanted to say he thought the same thing but thought he'd better stay humble and just say thanks. As the practice continued Chris was working on basic tackling drills. It seemed to go well until Coach Smith wanted Chris to work with the punt return and kick-off groups. As practice ended it seemed to Chris that things were a little different in that the coaches gave him a lot more attention.

The week went by quickly with classes and practice. Chris hardly saw Jessie all week except for their choir class. Friday morning came along and all the players had to wear their jerseys again to school. It was funny how some of the jerseys were still a little mud-stained from last Friday night even though they all had been washed. Sitting in study hall Chris could see the backs of the players and the stains still there that didn't quite get washed out. That was the case for a lot of the jerseys, but not number twenty-three, which was Chris's number. It was still bright white.

The game on Friday night would take place at St. Michael, Iowa. It was nearly forty miles away. When the team got there they all filed into the visiting locker room. It was a cloudy, cool day and the night air was even cooler. It also started to feel like it could rain. The pre-game warm ups were going fine but Chris was still uncertain whether he was going to get to play or not.

Then Coach Smith walked over to Chris and said, "Well New York, we're planning on using you a little bit tonight so stay alert."

The opening kick-off went to St. Michael and after they began their offense Coach Smith walked over to Chris and said, "Get your warm up off and get yourself loose."

Chris was very nervous and just kept watching the action on the field not knowing for sure what to expect. St. Michael failed to convert on third down so their punting unit came out onto the field. The Burton Bulldogs punt return unit also gathered on the field to receive the ball. Billy Snow, who was already on the field went back to prepare to receive the punt.

Chris looked over at the coach and asked, "Am I supposed to go in and receive the punt?"

The next voice heard was from the coach saying, "Hey Billy Snow, get out of there and over here on the bench."

Billy shook his head in disbelief and the coach slapped Chris on the back side and told him to get his butt out there. As Billy was running to the sidelines he purposely ran into Chris with his shoulder as Chris was trotting out onto the field.

As they hit one another Billy said to Chris, "I hope you drop the ball."

Chris didn't respond. When he lined up he realized he forgot his mouth guard. "Too late now," he thought.

When Chris heard the announcer saying, "Back to receive the punt for Burton is number twenty-three, Chris Williams," it gave him the shivers.

As the punt sailed in the air Chris realized he had lined up too deep. He quickly started running forward to get to the ball. As he caught the ball on a dead run he could see a defender running a little out of control trying to reach out for him, but he was unable to get a good grip on Chris. Chris saw another defender out of the corner of his eye who looked like he was going to lay Chris out flat, but Chris quickly darted to the left and then to the right. The would-be tackler only fell flat on his face as he tried to reach out and ended up grabbing a bunch of air.

Chris, with a full head of steam, started angling to the left and kept running full speed. He ran down the sidelines right past more tacklers and past the Burton Bulldogs bench as well as in front of the Burton fans on the sideline. No one from either team was within fifteen yards of him. Chris kept thinking, "Don't drop the ball, don't step out of bounds, and don't look back!" Chris scored his first touchdown with a seventy-two yard punt return that stunned everybody! Burton fans were on their feet screaming and clapping for joy. The St. Michael fans were silent.

The announcer was even a little stunned as he said, "Who is this kid?" He then said, "Wow, number twenty-three, sophomore, Chris Williams for the touchdown."

Burton went on to win that game by a score of forty-one to seventeen. Chris ran back three kick offs and five punts for twenty-three yards and one touchdown.

Chris thought to himself, "This may have been the most exciting night of my life!" After the game the coaches had a pep talk and singled out Chris for an outstanding performance. On the way home on the players' bus, everybody had something nice to say to Chris except Billy Snow. Chris sat with Elvis and Cory and they laughed and talked all the way home.

The next day Chris realized his left hand was swollen and felt jammed. When his mom discovered this she became very worried and concerned. She insisted they go to the clinic and get it checked out. The first thing Chris thought about was whether or not he could still play guitar. As the doctor examined his hand and then had it x-rayed, the frightful news was soon revealed. Chris had a slight fracture to a small bone in his left hand and it would have to be put in a cast for two to three weeks. Chris asked the doctor if he was certain, and of course, he was very certain.

This turned out to be a little more serious than he was prepared for. His mom said this was exactly what she feared with him playing football, but remembered that she had approved of him playing and knew that it made it easier for Chris to meet new friends.

When Chris's dad found out he was very disappointed for Chris. His dad called Coach Smith and told him the news. He too, was very disappointed. When the Coach found out his hand was in a cast he told Chris over the phone that it usually means the player is prohibited from playing in a game. He informed Chris that it was a state rule. The Coach did tell Chris he still wanted him at practice on Monday. Chris thought, "so much for being a football star." It lasted one night. There were only three games to go in the regular season and if the team could win two out of three of the remaining games, they could get to the play-offs.

Chris thought to himself, 'Now I can't play guitar or football.' He quietly and privately held his head and shed a few tears.

Saturday night was pretty quiet. No parties to play for or anything else really going on. Actually Chris was pretty sore and tired so Jessie came over and the two of them ended up watching a movie. As Chris gave thought to his injury and how or at what point in the game it happened, he started going over the events of the game beginning with the punt return for a touchdown. He thought it couldn't have happened then because he was barely touched by anybody. The next time he returned a punt he went about twenty-five yards and then stepped out of bounds. Then it came to him. On the next kick off, at the start of the second half, Chris recalled being forced out of bounds right at the St. Michaels sidelines and slammed into their wood bench. The officials called a penalty on St. Michaels for a late hit and they tacked on fifteen more yards to the return. It was the collision with the bench. Chris recalled being a little sore at the time but didn't think much of it. On the next kick return Chris remembered running all the way down to the fifteen yard line and being forced out of bounds but never being hit real hard, so it had to be the bench that caused the broken bone in his hand.

Jessie shared the excitement with Chris that she and all the fans felt watching Chris run so recklessly with the ball. She said it was a thrill for everybody to see Chris outrun so many of the tacklers. Jessie was just about as disappointed as he was about his injury. Not only because of his inability to play guitar but also because of the uncertainty of playing any more football this season.

On Sunday night Chris and Jessie once again went to church at the Lutheran youth service. When Chris and Jessie walked in they were greeted by Pastor Jim. He gave them a big smile and told Chris what a great game he had on Friday night. Chris replied by saying thank you and then showed the pastor the cast on his left hand. The pastor showed a sympathetic and pained expression. After Chris told the whole story of how it happened, the first question Pastor Jim had was, "What about your guitar?" Chris told him that everything was on hold for now.

Chapter Fourteen

Monday morning arrived and Chris was up and ready for school as always. Chris's dad was still at home before he left for school and tried to give Chris a little advice before heading out the door. He told him not to get too bigheaded at school over his success on the football field from last Friday night. He also said to enjoy the attention. Chris understood the advice that his dad shared with him but assured him that being arrogant or overconfident when he had a broken bone in his hand, and his season may already be over, was not going to happen.

When Chris walked into the school the first person he saw was Ms. Oman, the choir director.

She said, "Chris we are planning our Homecoming school dance in three weeks and I was wondering if you could gather up your group and play some music?"

Ms. Oman was unaware of Chris's injury to his hand. When he explained what happened and how long it was going to take to heal, it put a different turn on the plans Ms. Oman had for Chris playing guitar for the dance. She said she was very disappointed that it ever happened and was equally disappointed that Chris ever started playing football. Before she walked away she gave Chris a little squeeze on his forearm and said, "See you in choir." Her perfume lingered in Chris's head for the next few minutes.

Coach Smith called Chris out of study hall at third hour and asked if he could meet with him in his office. When they got together the coach told Chris how unfortunate it was that he had this injury but thanked Chris for an outstanding game on Friday night.

He said, "The local paper has contacted me and wanted to know some information about our new secret weapon from New York."

Coach Smith said he gave the paper a story that would be out that week. Coach then told Chris that he wanted him at every practice and expected him to stay in shape. The coach also had some therapy lined up for Chris to try and get that hand to heal quickly.

When Chris got to practice the guys gave him a hard time about getting hurt in his first game, but most of them were pretty nice about it. Coach Smith told Chris to put on all of his pads but not to participate in any of the contact drills, only running and leg strengthening activities. The coach also told him he wanted Chris in all of the team meetings. He said he wanted him in the weight room whenever he couldn't do any of the drills that might re-injure his hand. Chris wanted to know why he needed to put all of his pads on and the coach told him it was important to feel the weight of the pads at practice as he would at game time.

He then said, "Trust me kid, I know what I'm doing. We need to keep your head in this game so when you come back it won't feel so strange."

When Chris went home after practice he gave his mom the note about therapy. She said she'd call the clinic in the morning. Jessie came over and said she heard they were asked to play for the Homecoming dance. Chris said he didn't know if he could play with his hand like it was. He told Jessie not to make any plans yet until he started with some therapy at the clinic or hospital. Chris and Jessie went over to her house and worked on some vocal harmonies. Cory showed up later and also helped sing a little, as Jessie played the piano.

As it turned out Chris was not able to have any rehab or therapy for at least a week after the fracture. The rest of the week was pretty normal with school and football practice. The coach had made sure Chris kept up with the playbook. He had him be a part of their formations and understand the terminology. Chris was not too sure why, but he did whatever it took to learn what they were showing him on the offense. The team was preparing for the Pine City Tigers, a good football team with a great senior quarterback. His name was Tom Fountain.

As Friday drew nearer Chris felt a little distant from the football team knowing he could not play. The local paper was on the news stands on Thursday with a big story about the Burton's big win last Friday night. Chris felt a little uneasy about the story because it told all about the success he had last week but never mentioned his injury.

"I guess the coach didn't want that to be known yet," he thought.

On game night the coach told Chris to suit up and be on the bench with the team. Coach Smith's strategy was to force the other team to prepare for Chris not knowing when he would play.

The Burton Bulldogs played hard but were no match for the quarterback from Pine City. That kid could throw the ball with such ease. They beat the Bulldogs by a score of thirty-five to twenty. The season was down to two regular season games. In order to get to the play offs the Burton Bulldogs would have to win both games.

Chris started therapy on Tuesday of the next week. The doctors took the cast off and started working on strength and flexibility exercises. The therapist was surprised at the level of strength Chris had in his hand. Chris credited that to playing guitar. They told Chris he was ready for a soft removable support instead of the hard cast; however they told him he was not ready for football yet. He was also to take it easy on the guitar for a while. They did tell Chris that playing guitar a little might help speed his recovery.

So the next week Chris did start playing his guitar. Jessie, Cory and Karl came over to Chris's almost every night to play music. They would play only until Chris's hand became sore. Everybody had a good time playing and singing. Elvis came over a couple nights and reminded them that they still had to let him sing a song sometime soon.

Friday night rolled around and the football team looked good. They won on the road. Their opponent was Springfield. The Bulldogs seemed to recover from their loss the week before and played solid. Chris again watched from the sidelines and wished he could have played. The score was fourteen to ten.

The following week was Homecoming and Chris told Ms. Oman that they could play some songs but he also said they better be prepared to play recorded music just in case his hand wasn't healing up like he hoped it would. Ms. Oman told him they already had a D.J. booked to do part of the entertainment if need be. The whole week was pretty crazy with all the Homecoming activities. Spider Wilson and Elvis were up for homecoming king along with Joey Hamilton, the quarterback, and Billy Snow.

At practice the coach found out that Chris could be cleared to play because the cast had been removed. Coach asked Chris to get involved with a little contact and catching punts and kick-offs. The trainers taped up Chris's hand to protect it. Coach Smith also had Chris playing with the offense as a running back. They only had four plays for him to learn. Two to the right, and two to the left. The one play was a sweep right pitch and Chris would follow the quarterback, who would be the lead blocker. The same play was also used going to the left. The other play had Chris running between the guard and tackle. Going left Chris would run between Elvis and the guard, Don Thorton. They called him Woolly because his hair looked like a big old woolly sheep.

At practice, Elvis put an arrow on his butt in order to show Chris what direction he should run. The guard did the same thing. The coach didn't find much humor in it but he let it go. Each night the coach would have Chris spend about twenty minutes practicing these plays.

The coach kept telling Chris to be patient at the line of scrimmage and then, "Make your move to the opening." He kept preaching, "Don't turn on the speed until you are sure where the hole is going to open up. If you get ahead of yourself you're only going to run into the pile."

The doctors did clear Chris to play, but he was not sure what the coach had in mind for him so he didn't dare ask. The whole week of practice Chris caught punts and kick offs and spent a little time with the offense doing those same plays. Chris's evenings were spent practicing music with the guys and Jessie. Before he knew it, it was Friday. The school was decorated with all sorts of banners and the gym had balloons and crepe paper strung up all over the place for the homecoming dance. Chris was still trying to figure out if the coach was going to have him play in the offense on those four plays tonight or just what was going to happen. One guy who was not very happy about things was Billy Snow. The reason he was upset was because Chris was practicing in his position. It was only four plays but nevertheless, it was taking Billy out of the offense for those plays. This game was very important to win. Without a win the season would be over. With a win the team would be in the play offs and may be still in the hunt for the conference championship. That would depend on how some of the other teams ended up with wins and losses.

The opponent was the Carlton Spartans from Carlton, Iowa. They were the real deal, having a solid program for many years. They were the conference champs and state champions the last two years, and displayed signs on the edge of their town to let any travelers or local folks know. The town was very proud of their football team.

Chris had a nice surprise when he found out his sister was on her way from New York. She was supposed to arrive that Friday night and hopefully be in time for the game.

At game time the trainers taped up Chris's hand, but perhaps a little too much. Chris said he couldn't feel the ball the way he wanted to. The coach watched Chris field the punts during warm-ups and became a little concerned that he dropped a few. Chris's dad came down by the field and asked what the problem was. He tried to encourage Chris to focus more on just catching the ball. As the game was about to begin the air was cool and crisp with a slight breeze and it was just starting to sprinkle. It could be rough for Chris with his bad hand wrapped. He didn't need it to start raining, too.

Chris saw no action the entire first half. The Spartans received the opening kick and never punted the whole first half. The Spartans, after scoring two touchdowns did kick the ball to the Bulldogs. Billy Snow returned the kicks but with very little success. At half time the score was sixteen to seven in favor of the Spartans. By then the rain was coming down pretty heavy.

Quarterback Joey Hamilton fumbled the ball two times. Joey was a good player and a nice guy. It was a shame to see him have a bad night because of weather conditions. He had big blue eyes that went with his blond hair. For a quarterback, he was really built with big arms and a thick neck. He was well liked by all, especially the girls. At halftime the coach gave his usual speech to try to get his team ready for the second half.

The opening kick-off for the second half would be taken by the Burton Bulldogs. Billy Snow had been doing the kick return duties in the first half. The coach told Chris he wanted him ready to return the ball but with the rain coming down he wanted Billy Snow to catch the ball and pitch it to Chris.

"You follow his block Chris."

Chris responded by saying, "Yes, sir."

Chris was happy that he was finally going to get to play. He tried to loosen up by running and stretching at half time but he felt uneasy about getting back in the game again.

The official blew the whistle and the second half was about to begin. The coach was still going over details with Chris about letting Billy Snow catch the ball and pitch it back. He then said again to follow his block. As Chris strapped on his helmet and trotted onto the field there was a roar from the crowd cheering him on. Most of the fans remembered the great game Chris had just a few weeks ago against St. Michaels.

Then the announcer said, "Back deep to receive the kickoff is number twenty-three, Chris Williams."

As the kick sailed high in the air the rain reflected in the lights. For a few seconds as the ball was heading in his direction Chris could feel the tension that this moment presented. He thought for a moment that maybe Billy wouldn't give him the ball and keep it himself, but what happened was worse. Billy caught the ball and then hesitated for just a moment as if to put Chris in a defenseless situation. He pitched the ball back to Chris, who caught it cleanly, but as a defender was bearing down on him, Billy stepped aside and let the tackler absolutely level Chris. It was so obvious what Billy did, or didn't do. The whole stadium saw it. The collision was heard all the way up to the top of the bleachers. When the tackler hit Chris it knocked his helmet right off of him and Chris took a shot right above his left eye. Yet Chris was somehow able to hang on to the ball. As Chris lay on the ground it seemed to him as if the whole world became silent for just a few seconds. He could feel the wet ground soaking into the back of his head. Chris recalled seeing Billy move sideways but never saw the defender until he was in his face. The sound of the crunching was devastating but didn't hurt as bad as it sounded. Soon he could hear the sounds of the crowd murmuring and he could still feel the ball clutched against his mid section.

Coach Smith and the trainers came running out on the field right away. As they were standing over Chris they asked, "New York, are you OK?"

Chris said, "My left eye feels puffed up. Is it bleeding?"

The coaches and the trainers assured Chris there was no sign of blood coming from above his eye.

When Chris got up on his feet the whole crowd gave a sigh of relief and then some cheering and applause broke the silence in the stands. The coach told the trainers to look after Chris and then he turned to Billy Snow and yelled, "You're done!"

The whole crowd could hear the coach holler. Probably half the town could've heard him. The hush from the crowd was almost scary. As Chris walked back to get his helmet he realized he was just fine except his eye was about to become a big old shiner.

While Chris walked to the side lines he could still hear the coach yelling at Billy. The coach took a time out. When he cooled down a little he came over and asked Chris if he was OK and if he could play.

Chris said, "Yes I'm OK, but I'm not sure what you want me to do."

The coach said, "You will be taking Billy's spot. Those plays we worked on this week, can you run them?"

"Yes sir!"

Joey, the quarterback, was told what plays to run as Chris grabbed his helmet and ran out onto the field. The crowd once again responded with a big round of applause. In the huddle it was all business. Joey called out the play, "forty-two left on two."

As they started to line up Joey came over to Chris and said "You're going to get the ball and just follow your buddy Elvis on the left side."

On "two" the ball was snapped and Chris took the hand-off and waited for just a split second with a little stutter step and then saw a small seam on the left side. He shot through it just on the right side of Elvis' block. Chris ran straight past the defensive line and gained twleve yards before being tackled by one of the safeties.

The next play Joey called a left pitch on two. Once again Chris took the pitch from Joey and tried to find something out front but there was nothing there so he went wider to the left and got a great block from Joey, the quarterback. Also Cory the wide receiver gave him a nice little block to help spread the play out wide. Chris ran twenty-one yards down the sideline before being forced out of bounds. The next two plays were a fake pitch to Chris, and Joey kept the ball himself. Both plays picked up good yardage. The following two plays were called back because of penalties. Chris got a little too anxious and caused a false start on one play. The next play the right end did the same thing and it cost them another five yards.

Now it was second and twenty on the next play from the thirty-six yard line of the Carlton Spartans. With two more running plays it became fourth and two from the eighteen yard line. Normally Billy Snow would kick a field goal from this distance but tonight was different. Billy put on his helmet and started walking onto the field with the place kicking tee in his hand. Coach Smith told Billy to go sit down!

In the huddle Joey called a play that was a short pass over the middle that started with a fake handoff to Chris. Then Chris would try to break free and catch the short quick pass just behind the linebackers. The fullback was a great blocker but did not run the ball much, so he was supposed to stay back and help protect Joey as he attempted to throw the ball.

Joey said to Chris, "They'll never suspect you as a receiver. This should work to get the first down." Joey then told Chris, "You can do this. It's just like catching a real short punt."

On "one" the ball was hiked and the team sold the fake to Chris. They sold it so well that they thought Chris had the ball, he was tackled and ended up on the ground. Chris managed to quickly jump up and saw that Joey was still scrambling, so Chris put his hands up in the air.

He was about nine to ten yards down field. Joey threw a bullet and Chris caught the ball but it bounced out of his hands and into mid air. It may have actually bounced off Chris's shoulder pads. The closest defender made an attempt to catch the ball off of the deflection, but somehow

Chris was able to grab the ball out of the arms of the defender. Chris held on to it tightly and twisted around to try and find some room to run and discovered the linebacker had fallen down. The safety was out of position and it left a wide open lane for Chris to turn on the speed. Chris outran everybody heading towards the end zone and then easily crossed the goal line for a touchdown! The whole team enjoyed the roar of the crowd cheering. The two point attempt unfortunately failed on a quick pass to the left because it was batted down. The score was Bulldogs thirteen, Carlton sixteen.

The third quarter ended after both teams had failed to score any more points. Chris returned one punt in the third quarter but only for a short gain. The fourth quarter was a grind-it-out fight for both teams. After nearly a six minute drive by the Spartans, they fumbled the ball on the Bulldogs' twelve yard line. Cory forced the fumble and recovered it himself. This was a huge break for the Bulldogs. With only about two minutes left Coach Smith came over to Chris and asked him if his eye was doing ok. He also asked how his hand was feeling at the same time. By this time Chris's eye was just about swollen shut. Chris told the coach he was just fine and went back on the field.

The biggest problem Chris had was not knowing all the plays. Chris looked back at the bench and noticed Billy Snow sitting all by himself. As they began the drive down the field, the first play was to the senior wide out Jason

Carter who caught the ball over the middle and rambled down the field for almost twenty yards. The team regrouped with no huddle. Joey Hamilton walked over to Chris and told him on two, pitch right and just follow the block. As Chris lined up he realized that he could hardly see out of his left eye and his left hand was getting a little sore. A light rain was still falling and the night air was cooling down. When the ball was snapped, Joey handed it off to Chris. Joey was the lead blocker on this play, but he was cut down as soon as he got the ball to Chris. Chris quickly realized there was nowhere to go on the right side without Joey blocking, so he changed directions and went to the left. The wet field left some of the defenders slipping and sliding trying to change direction with Chris. When Chris was able to start running he found an open field in front of him and turned on his speed until one of the deep backs from the Spartans got an angle on him and forced him out of bounds. All in all Chris ran nearly forty yards before he was stopped.

The Bulldogs were on the Spartans' twenty-eight yard line with about a minute left and the clock stopped. The next play was a screen pass to Cory, who played wide receiver on offense. Cory ended up putting the Bulldogs on the nine yard line before they were stopped. Coach Smith called a time out and ran on the field. After some short inspiring words of encouragement, next came the play from the coach. He called the play where Chris would run between Elvis and Woolly, the two offensive linemen who had the arrows drawn on their butts during practice. It also required the fullback to be the lead blocker just ahead of Chris. The whistle blew from the officials and the time out was over.

As the team assembled for the next play the rain stopped a little but the field was muddy at this end. Joey called out the cadence for the play. Chris could feel the butterflies in his stomach and his knees were shaking a little. The pitch came back to Chris and he started following the fullback but before he could even get started, he got pulled down from behind for a one yard loss. Time was running out so the Bulldogs called their last time out. In the huddle Joey called the same play again on two.

He leaned over to Chris with an attempt to pump him up and said "New York, we need you to do your magic."

During the time out, Elvis and Woolly, being just a little bit cute, took some of the mud from the wet field and put arrows on their butts to show Chris where to run. Elvis had the arrow pointing to the right on his butt and Woolly, the left guard, had his arrow on his butt facing to the left. It was just like they did as a joke at practice with a magic marker, only this time it was done with the mud from the field. Chris couldn't help but to chuckle a little. He was thinking how cool those guys remained under such pressure. Joey took the snap and handed it off to Chris and he followed the fullback between the arrows on the back ends of the two linemen and found a lane that took him towards a Spartans' linebacker who was waiting to tackle Chris. As Chris approached the tackler he stutter stepped just enough to freeze the linebacker and Chris stumbled and twisted enough to break free and jump over one of the defenders near the ground. Chris kept his legs pumping and moving forward, as water and mud from the ground splashed upward on his legs. He then twisted his body to avoid another tackler and after nearly falling down, was still able to somehow stumble his way through, completely off balance and then into the end zone! As he tumbled into the end zone, mud and water splashed up and covered Chris's uniform and his face. The officials signaled touchdown! The Bulldogs were so excited they piled on Chris. The crowd was as loud as they'd been all night, screaming and jumping up and down. The bleachers were moving up and down. Chris finally got up from the bottom of the pile of Bulldog players swarming all over him and he walked over to the referee and handed him the ball like a total gentlemen. At this point you could not read number twenty-three on the front or back of his jersey and the mud was dripping off of his facemask. Then he trotted to the bench with one hand slightly in the air as to say, humbly, thank you to the roaring crowd. The coach handed him a towel as he walked to the sidelines. Chris tried to clean off his face from the mud. Then the coach gave him a big slap on the backside and a big hug.

The crowd from Burton was on its feet and cheering for number twenty-three, Chris Williams. The Bulldogs went for the two point conversion with a quarterback sneak. It worked! They hung on with very little time left in the game for a win. The final score was twenty-one to sixteen. It was such a big victory because it meant that the Bulldogs still had a chance to win the conference championship, depending on how the other team standings came out. It did mean that they were in the playoffs for sure. Carlton and Burton were neighboring towns and lately Carlton had been on the winning side of things more so than Burton.

The celebration on the field was great. The whole team was jumping around and hugging each other. The fans didn't want to leave even though the rain was still coming down in a cold drizzle. The school band was on the sidelines and started playing some good pep tunes. Raindrops reflected on the bell of the tuba, played by Mike Murphy. He may have been the best tuba player the school has ever had. You could hear his horn all the way up town. It sounded great! Another loud and good player friend was Eddie Carletti. They called him "Eddie Spaghetti". His saxophone cut through the air, along with one of the other sax players "Coco-Mo Joe".

The locker room was festive! Coach Smith was good at praising his players and getting them to play hard and pointing out the guys who really put in extra effort. He especially made nice comments about Chris, Joey

Hamilton, Cory and the entire offense. He praised the defense for not allowing any points to be scored in the entire second half. He then pointed out that Chris had eighty yards rushing in the second half with two touchdowns, one pass completion, a punt return and one not so good kick-off return. He then said that most of this was done with one eye nearly swelled shut and one sore left hand.

"Not bad for a shy kid from New York!" Then he said, "Thank you everybody! Go out and have a good and safe night!"

After the game Chris couldn't wait to see Jessie and his Mom and Dad. He was also hoping that his sister might be home then. When Chris came out from the locker room, his hair was still a little wet from his shower. He was quickly met by his mom and dad and Jessie. Standing behind them was his sister. Before anybody else had a chance, Vickie came around and gave Chris a great big hug with tears in her eyes. She told him she missed the first half but watched him play the rest of the game.

She said, "I miss you Chris, and brother you were great!"

This was followed by a huge hug from the other three. Everybody, including Ben had tears of joy and perhaps relief, until Cindy, Chris's mother saw the big shiner on Chris's left eye. Then she wasn't so joyful. Chris looked like a boxer who just went fifteen rounds. He told his mother it didn't hurt and asked her to just let him enjoy the moment. Chris's dad laughed and shook his head.

Jessie and Chris walked to the gym where the D.J. was set up and already playing several great songs. Alongside of his equipment was all the band gear that the guys set up right after school. Soon after, Cory and Elvis came in showing a little wear and tear from the game as well. Elvis just looked a little worn down but Cory had a bit of a limp to his walk. Both guys could not stop smiling in spite of being beat up from a hard fought game. Karl was right behind them holding his sticks and ready to play at anytime. All the guys had a few laughs about the game and about the arrows on the back sides of Elvis and Woolly. They were told by Ms. Oman that they could play about forty five minutes or so but not until after the coronation of the Homecoming King and Queen. After a little while Ms. Oman announced that the candidates for Queen and King should come to the stage area. There was a short ceremony and soon they crowned the new royalty. Joey Hamilton was crowned as the new King and Sally Jefferson, who was the head cheerleader, was crowded as the new Queen. They were popular students and the most likely to become the new royalty.

The band finally got to play, and the crowd was ready for some good live music! The dance floor filled up in no time. Chris started off with a medley of some good rock 'n' roll oldies with his Fender Stratocaster guitar cranked up.

Jessie and Cory's voices along with Karl singing nice low harmonies were right in tune with Chris's lead voice. Karl was pounding out a beat that could be heard two blocks away. He loved to push his snare drum volume as much as he dared and it sounded great in the old gym. After Chris finished his medley of some oldies he kicked off the intro to a Johnny Cash song called "Folsom Prison Blues". He had a little distortion on his guitar and set his guitar pickups to get a brighter sound. The guitar had so much energy that it penetrated the walls of the gym. When Chris finished the short intro and hit the "E" chord, Karl started singing the lead vocals. His low voice resembled the sound of Johnny Cash. Chris had learned the correct guitar lines from listening to the original record and enjoyed playing his parts. Johnny Cash would be proud! Cory's bass guitar cut through like a knife as the low end just rocked. You could feel the beat in your chest as the music moved everybody. It was absolutely magic. Elvis was out front trying to listen to help them get a good balance level. It wasn't long before he came up to the stage and gave the thumbs up with a big smile. It was so fun for everybody!

The mood was right with the music playing and the team having won the game. The band played about six songs and then Jessie announced they had a special guest star coming up to sing. This was news to Chris. He wondered who was going to come on stage. They brought up Elvis to finally do a song. Chris hadn't known that Jessie had worked with

Elvis a little through the week and had him prepared to sing an old Elvis Presley song called "Hound Dog". They had the key worked out and were ready to surprise Chris. When he got on stage he did a couple of Elvis Presley dance moves right away and really entertained the crowd.

Cory hollered out, "Elvis is in the building!"

Elvis then grabbed the microphone and waited for a moment for Jessie to hit a "C" chord on the piano to give him his pitch. Then Elvis kicked off the song and the crowd went crazy. This only inspired him more, and he really laid it on thick with the dance moves and twisting and turning his hips as much as he could. His pitch was not perfect but his craziness made up for any wrong notes or words he missed. He was really entertaining.

When he finished, Cory hollered out, "Ladies and gentlemen, Elvis has left the building!"

The crowd went nuts! Chris enjoyed it more than anyone else. The whole dance was so much fun. The dance was almost over when the Burton Bulldogs found out that they were the conference champs after learning that Kellogg had lost their game that night. This left the Bulldogs with the best record in the conference. What a great night of celebration for everybody.

Chapter Fifteen

When school started on Monday Chris showed up to his first hour classes with a very noticeable black eye. The kids in school gave him a hard time about it but it was all in good fun. Billy Snow met Chris in the hallway and just stared him down with an angry look. Chris, with sarcasm, stopped and stared right back at him as if to say, you don't scare me one bit. Then Chris just sort of smiled and kept walking.

At football practice after school, the coach was all business. The first thing the coach did was congratulate the team for winning the conference. His next goal was to prepare the team for the upcoming playoff game. At this point the coach was very serious.

In the practice Chris played a little bit at safety on the defense. Their next opponent was Jefferson High. They were told Jefferson had a lot of speed on offense and were undefeated this season. They were also favored to win it all this year.

On one of the formations at practice, Chris was on defense playing safety and was told by the defensive coordinator, Mr. Woll to crowd the line of scrimmage. When the ball was snapped he wanted Chris to rush the quarterback, Joey Hamilton. As Chris walked up to the line of scrimmage the tight end angled just a little in order to try and block Chris. When they snapped the ball Chris ran right past the tight end and headed with a full head of steam to the backfield. Joey handed the ball off to Billy Snow and Chris met Billy head on and took Billy completely off both his feet and drove him right into the ground. The collision could have been heard two blocks away. Billy gasped and grunted as he got hit by Chris. Chris was at absolute full speed when they met and Chris put his shoulders right into the chest of Billy Snow. It was a legal hit. With Chris's speed, it seemed as if Billy got hit by a train! As Billy laid there moaning the coaches came over to see if he was ok. Billy slowly got up and then fell down. As he went to one knee, he was still woozy from the thrashing he just took. With the help of the coaches, he struggled to get to his feet again. Blood was coming from his mouth that turned out to be nothing more than him biting his tongue or lip. He again went down to the ground like a fighter who just had his clock cleaned. Chris stood over him and thought, "Come on big guy, you're not so tough now!"

When Billy could finally speak he took off his helmet while still laying on the ground, looked at Chris and said, with a weak voice, "Nice hit, New York, I guess I had that one coming." He then tried to wipe off the blood from the side of his mouth.

Chris took his helmet off and Billy stood up. They were face to face and Chris had no intentions of backing off while looking Billy right in the eye. Billy brought up his right hand to shake Chris's hand. With much hesitation Chris slowly stuck out his hand to shake and then heard Billy repeat, "Nice hit" and walked slowly to the water cooler with a bit of a limp and a stagger to his walk. Chris was surprised and a little relieved that just maybe the feud between them was finally over.

He remembered what his dad had said. Don't take any crap and don't give any crap. Coach Smith heard and saw the whole incident and just smiled and winked at Chris.

Then the coach walked over to Billy to make sure he was ok and put his arm around him while shaking his head and said, "Billy I hope you learned a little something from this."

That week of practice was very serious with the coaches trying to get the team prepared for a big challenge in the first round of the play offs. The game was on Thursday night.

In spite of a great effort by the Burton Bulldogs, the Jefferson Raiders were a little too much for the Bulldogs to handle. Jefferson had a great team with a fast paced offense that kept the Bulldogs slightly off balance most of the night. Billy Snow was back in good graces with the coach and played the game at linebacker and did the place kicking duties as usual. Billy also started at running back. Chris shared the running back position with Billy. Chris had some nice runs totaling nearly seventy-five yards and one touchdown. Chris also returned one punt for a near touchdown but was forced out of bounds after running over fifty yards down the sideline. The Bulldogs' defense was solid but just couldn't stop the Raiders on third down. The final score was Jefferson twenty-four and the Burton Bulldogs twenty.

Coach Smith had a great message as he addressed the team in the locker room after the game. He thanked the players for their effort and said he was very proud of everybody and pointed out, even though they didn't win, being the conference champs was nothing to sneeze at. The Jefferson Raiders went on to win the state championship. They deserved to be the champs because they were a class act.

Epilogue

As for Chris, he sat down over the weekend and thought about what a disappointment it was that they didn't win the game, but realized what a great season it had been and what a great experience it was for him. How a bashful kid from New York, who only knew the arts and music, found himself as an athlete on a pretty good football team. He thought about how he discovered he had talents he never knew he had. If he hadn't been forced to move to Iowa, he might never have had the chance to play sports. He also realized he would've never met Jessie. Thank God for Jessie! He also thought about the good friends he met all because of Jessie, and the music and football all revolved around these new friends. Also how he became friends with Pastor Jim and what he had said about the power of music.

Wow it was so true! Music was the energy that fueled most of this to happen.

Chris also thought that he never would have done any of these things if he hadn't been brave enough to step out of his comfort zone and try something different. He realized that living in Burton Iowa wasn't so bad. As it turns out, its slower pace and peaceful values were very refreshing and resembled a time when our world wasn't so crazy.

Chris was excited to move on to the next season of football and maybe even go out for track. He had already been approached by the track coach, Mr. Woll who was also the assistant football coach, about joining the team in the spring.

He felt his music had some promise and it was still his real passion. He loved singing and playing music more than anything else in the whole world. Ms. Oman has already persuaded Chris to take a lead part in the all-school play in the winter. Chris truly appreciated the opportunity to play music and also football with some new-found friends and was very grateful to his teachers, coaches and teammates. He was excited about the upcoming season of football and the many new seasons of life, and all the adventures they hold.

The End

Mike Murtha

About the Author

Mike Murtha

I was born and raised in a small town in western Wisconsin. My creative background is in performing music as well as writing songs. I am also a sign painter. I did find some similarities in writing a novel and writing songs. As I wrote my story I would often think what you have to do to keep an audience, or in this case a reader. This resembles the feeling of performing music to a live audience. I've been a semi professional musician for nearly forty years. Thank God I never quit my day job! I have been fortunate in my musical career to have played with some real professionals. I hope you enjoy my first attempt at being a novel writer.